STRANGE
EXIT

STRANGE EXIT

PARKER PEEVYHOUSE

TOR TEEN

A TOM DOHERTY ASSOCIATES BOOK

NEW YORK

STRANGE EXIT

Copyright © 2019 by Parker Peevyhouse

Designed by Greg Collins

A Tor Teen Book
Published by Tom Doherty Associates
120 Broadway
New York, NY 10271

www.tor-forge.com

Tor® is a registered trademark of Macmillan Publishing Group, LLC.

Library of Congress Cataloging-in-Publication Data

Names: Peevyhouse, Parker, author.
Title: Strange exit / Parker Peevyhouse.
Description: First edition. | New York : Tor Teen, 2020.
Identifiers: LCCN 2019041384 (print) | LCCN 2019041385 (ebook) |
    ISBN 9780765399427 (hardback) | ISBN 9780765399441 (ebook)
Subjects: CYAC: Virtual reality—Fiction. | Computer simulation—Fiction. |
    Science fiction.
Classification: LCC PZ7.1.P444 (print) | LCC PZ7.1.P444 (ebook) |
    DDC [Fic]—dc23
LC record available at https://lccn.loc.gov/2019041384
LC ebook record available at https://lccn.loc.gov/2019041385

Our books may be purchased in bulk for promotional, educational, or business use. Please contact your local bookseller or the Macmillan Corporate and Premium Sales Department at 1-800-221-7945, extension 5442, or by email at MacmillanSpecialMarkets@macmillan.com.

First Edition: January 2020

Printed in the United States of America

0 9 8 7 6 5 4 3 2 1

For my sister, Gwynne, for bravely reading everything
I've written since I could hold a pencil

STRANGE

EXIT

1

LAKE

The San Francisco Zoo: gates rusted open, weeds bursting through cracks in the asphalt, trees like many-armed scarecrows, broken and stunted. Lake figured she was the only person to set foot in the place in years. Not counting the boy in the tiger exhibit.

Lake peered in at him through a curtain of dirt over the viewing glass. She guessed he was around her age, seventeen. He sat on a log, hunched over something she couldn't see. No tiger in sight. Was it wandering the abandoned zoo, looking for snacks like Lake was looking for people to rescue? Lake shivered. *Hope not.* Because that would mean she and the tiger were looking for the same thing.

Lake scanned the ash-gray landscape, the shattered dead trees. Checked the other big cat exhibits. Went and listened at the cracked-open doors of the Lion House. No sign of anyone other than the boy in the tiger yard.

How was she going to get him out? She could go stand at the glass that shielded the exhibit and shout across the moat.

But she'd long ago discovered that barriers made everyone more feral, no matter which side they were on.

She could scrape herself up climbing over the fake rocks that ringed the exhibit. Kind of a hot day for something that dangerous. That left the door at the back of the exhibit, which would mean going through the Lion House. Couldn't still be lions in there after so many years, right? They'd either be dead or roaming free—not lying in wait. But that was the kind of thing people said right before they broke into a lion house and got mauled.

She pulled at the back of her shirt, which was starting to stick. She was spending too much time here. There were other people holed up in other parts of the city, groups of them who needed her to tell them that it was time to come out. He was only one person.

But he was stuck, same as the others were.

Lake patted the flank of a bronze lion sculpture that lay toppled on the steps. "Wish me luck." The sculpture was green with verdigris, nested in pooled dirt. Real lucky.

Something tawny emerged from between the doors of the Lion House. Lake almost toppled over the felled sculpture in her rush to back away.

It was only a dog, a yellow Lab speckled with dirt. Lake's heart battered her rib cage for another minute, then quit being dramatic. "Hey, there." Lake eased forward and held out her hand. The dog panted. It wasn't half as skinny as Lake would have expected it to be. "Someone's been taking care of you."

The dog thumped its tail but wouldn't come closer. "Come here. Please?" Lake said. "It's been a rough day. Month."

Wandering empty neighborhoods and now an empty zoo.

"Promise I'm friendly." Lake stepped forward, but the dog turned and vanished through the doors.

You always rush it, Lake told herself. *With people, too.*

She stepped toward the doors, envisioning great cats crouching in the darkness. But then, the dog didn't seem to sense danger.

She pushed into the darkness, smelled mildew but no fetid breath. Heard the dog trotting off. "Wait, buddy. Wait for me."

Her eyes adjusted to the low light, and she went after a tawny blur that she hoped was the Lab, past rusted barriers, through open doors with their locks thrown back. Sunlight streamed through the doorway to the tiger yard. Lake went through and then closed the door behind her, even though it protested with a rusty squeal. She needed it shut, for later.

The light stung her eyes. Before her, a weird Eden: stunted trees, yellow-green grass struggling up through dirt, a thorny bush clawing its way out of the moat. The boy was wrestling the bush now, hacking at a green branch with a hunting knife. The dog supervised from the scant shade of a broken stump.

The boy stopped mid-hack to look Lake over, head to boots, eyes sharp like he expected her to have a weapon. Which she didn't. Well, except desperation, which was still no match for a hunting knife.

He didn't seem surprised to see her. Lake took that as a good sign. He must know that he didn't belong in this place. He must know someone would come to take him away.

He didn't say anything. His hand shook.

"Your dog invited me in," Lake finally said, trying not to stare at the knife. "He said something about lemonade."

No smile from the boy. No one appreciated humor anymore.

He wiped sweat from his brow with his free hand, which was still shaking. "You're wasting your time here."

Probably. But what's new?

He was half a foot taller than Lake. And, you know, had a knife. Seemed distraught. Lake inched backward. "You live here?" She looked around at the new grass, and the gray dirt that must have once been completely covered in greenery, before nuclear winter. The exhibit was so much bigger on the inside than it looked from the outside. "I've always wanted to go inside a tiger pen."

"Most people don't. That's why I came here. Safer." He went back to struggling with the bush.

"Safe from what?"

"People who might want to rob me. Beat me up. Ask me lots of questions while I'm busy."

Lake smiled. "That last bit was a joke, wasn't it? What a relief. I was afraid those didn't exist anymore."

He turned to look at her again, eyes half-lost in overgrown hair. He frowned like he didn't know what to make of her.

Lake pulled her shirt away from her sweaty back again. *How long have I been here now?*

Don't rush it.

"No tigers around?" she asked.

"Just its bones." He gave her an uncertain look. "I buried them."

Lake's stomach shrank. She glanced at the grass-studded dirt. At the boy again, his troubled gaze. He'd bothered to hold a funeral for a tiger—there was something promising in that. "Nice of you."

He shrugged. "Every time I looked at those bones, they made me think of . . ."

They both knew. "Death. The war."

Impact fires and nuclear winter.

"Didn't you hear? That's all over now." Lake looked up at the gray-blue sky. "The sun's out, the actual *sun*. Grass is growing. And all tigers are buried."

He gave her a brief smile. She felt it like warmth from the sun overhead.

"There must be better places to camp out than a tiger yard," Lake said. "Seems lonely here." *For one thing.* The smell of mud and sulfur wafted from the swampy moat.

The boy nodded at the dog. "I've got him, at least. Found him wandering."

Lake moved toward the dog, and this time it let her put a hand on its head. So nice to feel fur and floppy ears, to see its pink tongue. She missed dogs.

"You ever think of leaving?" She took a step toward the boy. He stood straighter, his collarbone jutting, like he didn't want her to come closer.

I'm rushing it.

A folded blanket lay on a log nearby, along with a metal cup and a pocket-tin. Lake nudged open the tin. Inside lay two cherry-red cough drops. "Are you saving these?"

The boy eyed them like he might pounce on her if she took one. Lake couldn't think of anything she wanted less. She'd only been curious.

"Yes," he said.

"What for?" Lake asked.

"My birthday."

"One for you, and one for the dog?"

The boy shrugged. "One for me and one for . . . whoever might come along."

Lake's heart sped up. This could work. She could do this.

"Just been waiting for someone to wander into your tiger yard?" she asked.

He turned to the bush, wielding his knife. "First I went to my house, to look for my parents." The branch he'd been working at finally separated from the bush, like a leg at a joint. He tossed the thorny mass into the moat. "They weren't there."

A bruising pain blossomed in Lake's chest. "I searched my own house, once. It was horrible inside. Everything covered in a layer of dust like a new hide."

The boy nodded. "All the food in my house was expired. Only the cough drops seemed any good. Weird what lasts and what doesn't."

Weird wasn't the word Lake would have used.

"I searched for my sister." She toyed with the bracelet on her wrist, a knotted blue thread. "Searched almost the whole city. But . . ."

The boy turned to her, looked like he'd just been punched. The knife fell to the dirt. "You didn't find her?"

"I found plenty of other people. You, for example."

The boy stared at the knife in the dirt.

Is this working?

Under Lake's fingers, notches in the lid of the tin said the boy had been counting the days he'd been waiting for someone to come along. "I always thought it was sad, seeing tigers locked up in zoos."

"Why? One tiger in a zoo probably saves a hundred in the wild. Anyway, zoos usually get the wounded ones. The ones that can't survive on their own." He pressed his hands together, and his fingers came away blood-streaked from the thorn-pricks on his palm.

"I think sometimes they let them back into the wild," Lake said. "When they're ready." *Are you ready?*

He looked down at his blood-spotted hands. "My birthday was two days ago."

That pain in her chest again, hollowing her out. One day, there'd be a hole where her heart was now.

Maybe she should stop coming to places like this.

But then—who else would?

She held out the tin to the boy. "Sorry I'm late."

She watched his face while he stared at the tin. Watched his expression change.

He took the tin from her.

I didn't rush it. That was a relief.

He turned away, and Lake felt a small burst of panic, but then she saw what he was doing. The branch he had cut off had revealed a cluster of deep red berries. The first fruit Lake had seen in ages. She went weak all over.

The boy twisted off the cluster and turned back to her.

"Berries so wild they have to be locked in a pen?" She smiled at the strangeness of it.

He smiled back. "Berries instead of tigers. Not a bad trade."

Lake pulled off a berry and ate it, and it was so tart she could have cried. The best berry she'd ever eaten.

The boy ate one too, plucking it with his red-stained fingers. Lake picked up the hunting knife from the dirt while he chewed. She strode to the back of the yard before he could protest.

She used the knife to scratch an X in the door there. Then she opened the door and held it for the boy like she was inviting him into the Land of the Lion House. Still holding the knife, which felt creepy, so she dropped it into the dirt.

The boy studied her a long moment like he knew the door would lead to somewhere other than the Lion House. "What happens when I walk through?"

"You stop living alone in a tiger yard."

He gave her a searching look. Blood and berry juice stained his hands and his jeans where he'd tried to wipe his hands clean. Like evidence of a pact they'd made.

He'll walk through.

He looked like he wanted to ask another question, so Lake smiled, waiting. "I'm sorry you didn't find your sister," he said.

Lake's smile faltered.

The boy walked through the door.

Lake stood alone in the yard, picturing Willow's crooked smile. Then she gave the place one last glance, blew a kiss to the dog, and stepped through.

The next moment, she was lying in a bed, staring up at a metal ceiling.

She gave herself a minute to come to her senses. Dull gleam

of steel, stale smell of recycled air, hum of generators. *You were in the simulation. Now you're out.*

And then the next realization hit her, same as it always did: *No Willow.*

But she had saved that boy. Relief ballooned inside her. He'd had a knife and was camped in a tiger yard, and she'd still convinced him to leave with her.

She wished she could have brought the dog through too, but it wasn't real, just a figment of the simulation.

She slipped her head out of the nest of wires and nodes, easing her temples past the touch-points. The plastic shell lifted and she pushed her legs over the side of the bed. Fumbled for the lock on the steel panel that opened the tiny room.

Beyond: rows and rows of more steel pods in a vast warehouse lit by flickering lights. Lake found her way through the maze to the warehouse's wide doorway, registering the hiss of air vents and the rumble of labored machinery that kept the ship running.

She stepped out into the smell of dirty clothes, farmed algae, desperation. *Welcome home.*

2

LAKE

Lake followed the arrows her fellow passengers had scratched into the ship's walls. Most of the ship's hallways led to locked doors, pitch-black rooms, groaning machinery, barricades of smashed supply crates. Some led to dorms or toilets, or to makeshift workshops strewn with broken bots, or to banks of red-flashing panels Lake had long ago given up trying to decipher. The arrows passengers left for one another were the only way to stay oriented.

Lake's stomach was begging for food, but she couldn't stop herself from doing this—searching. *Willow's not here,* she told herself. *She's not on the ship.*

She had to prove it to herself every time she woke up.

Somewhere in these hallways, the boy she had rescued from the simulation must be stumbling along, weak from stasis. Someone had probably already found him and was taking him to get food and water. Lake would check on him later.

She ended up at a locked door and then decided to go back

and scratch a mark to warn others about the dead end. She used a screw from a dissembled bot to do it. A girl heading out of a dorm room shot Lake a suspicious look. "Someone should make a map," Lake said lightly, but the girl hurried past. Everyone on the ship acted like they were still coming out of the fog of sleep, still trying to shake some bad dream.

Lake's stomach grumbled again. *Okay, I get it. Time for the eatery.*

At the end of the next hallway, the eatery buzzed with skittish energy, as always. It was the place most passengers hung out, hungry or not. Lake wouldn't call it crowded, exactly, considering it was meant to service a few hundred more people than had managed to get on board. But even with its tall view-screens and high ceiling it felt cramped, full of nerves and hunger and grumbling voices.

Lake kept her head down when she walked in, avoiding huddles of passengers who'd staked out their usual tables, where they played poker with makeshift cards, or went through all the same arguments over how to fix wheezing air vents and divvy up protein bars. Might have been a different scene if the passengers hadn't all been underage—but that was something Lake tried not to think about too much, the whole pied piper situation.

Scrawled all over the walls of the eatery were names of passengers lost to the simulation. Lake had been checking the names off one by one. Ninety-seven check marks. Only fifty-three left to go. Fifty-two, now.

And where were they all? It used to be easy to find people in the sim, even if it was hard to get them out. Now, she was more likely to find empty landscapes. Where in the sim could fifty-two people be hiding?

The eatery's overhead lights flickered.

Meanwhile, the ship's getting worse every day.

"Where are *you* coming from?" a boy barked at her as she tried to edge past his table.

Kyle. He'd been in Lake's government class back home, where she'd barely noticed him. Now, she couldn't avoid him—he liked to stand on tables and bark orders at people, as if studying power structures qualified him to create his own. He glared at her, arms crossed so he could show off his muscles in his ship-issue shirt.

"Catching up on my sleep," she said.

He caught her arm as she tried again to walk past. "You didn't go back into the sim?"

It was all she could do not to yank free. Eager as she was to escape his sweat-and-algae smell, she couldn't afford to fight Kyle. He was known for shoving people into the private dining rooms that ringed the eatery and served as makeshift holding cells. "Always out, never in," she said, the stupid motto everyone kept repeating. "Otherwise, we all just keep getting stuck." She forced a smile.

Kyle squinted at her.

Dummy—how do you think you got out of the sim? If I hadn't gone back in and found you barricaded in a school closet . . .

He was still gripping her arm, trying to decide if she was hiding something.

"Got anything to eat?" she asked, still smiling.

He let go of her arm like it was burning hot. "Sorry. Check the other tables."

Worked every time.

Lake found a chair at a mostly empty table and reached into the food box there. Empty. Her stomach complained.

A young girl sitting across the table silently chewed a protein bar. Lake had rescued this girl from the sim days ago. A week ago? Hard to keep track of time on a failing ship. She'd found the girl in an empty house, waiting for parents who would never come.

Was she any better off now, waiting to leave the ship?

The girl broke off half the protein bar she was eating and held it out to Lake.

Lake hesitated, surprised. "Thanks." She tapped her half against the girl's. "Cheers."

The girl was maybe thirteen—Willow's age. Eyes held that same challenge and curiosity. Probably had strong opinions on which music was the worst, which books the best, which Pop-Tart flavors were better cold or hot. Lake was willing to hear it all.

"You remember me?" Lake asked her. *Is that why you're sharing your food?*

The girl shrugged. "Sure. You come in here, sit by yourself. Leave alone."

Lake winced. "But you don't remember . . ." Of course she didn't remember Lake rescuing her. Lake was always careful to change her appearance when she went into the sim. Otherwise, people like Kyle would catch on and lock her up. "Never mind." Disappointment mingled with the loneliness Lake thought she had done so well at squashing.

She shifted her attention to the view-screens. "Best view

around." She gazed at the glowing curve of Earth and imagined herself looking through tall panel-windows. White swirling clouds, as beautiful from above as they had been from below.

Her throat ached at the thought.

How much longer until I'm under them?

"He likes it too," the girl said, and Lake shifted in her seat to see who the girl was pointing to.

The boy from the tiger yard.

Someone had shut him into a private dining room currently serving as a makeshift holding cell. He stood with a shoulder pressed against the glass door, staring at the distant view-screen, trembling so hard it was a wonder the glass didn't shake. Fresh out of stasis, and no one had bothered to feed him.

He caught her staring. Raised one shaking hand to press against the glass.

Lake looked away, rattled. But he couldn't have recognized her. He only wanted help.

She couldn't give it to him. She was trying to keep off everyone's radar. *Sorry.* She'd rescued him from one cage only to get him locked in another.

She chanced another quick look. He was so weak. *Don't do it,* she told herself.

But she got up and slinked to a drink dispenser. *Hope he likes algae smoothies. Nothing quite like the feeling that you're drinking a fish.* He wouldn't be able to keep much more down. He'd been getting all his meals through an IV.

She set the drink on the table someone had pushed in front

of his cell to barricade it shut. Then she dragged the table from the door, wincing at the squeal of metal scraping over metal.

"What are you doing?" someone barked.

Kyle again. He strode over, his glare undercutting her sense of accomplishment at budging the table.

"Did you ever have a pet?" Lake mustered the nerve to keep dragging the table. The boy behind the glass stood straighter, watching her progress with wide eyes. "You know how they die when you don't feed them?"

Kyle shoved the table back toward the door. "He'll be fine for a few hours. Take the fight out of him."

"Fight? He obviously *just* got out of the sim."

"The new ones always try to go right back in."

Lake glanced at the boy trapped behind safety glass. Skinny and sad. They always looked like that when they first woke up. It almost made her feel sorry for saving them. "So you're going to keep him in there until . . . ?"

"Until I feel like letting him out," Kyle said. "He gets trapped in the sim again, we're that much worse off."

"So explain it to him." Lake turned to the boy behind the glass. She owed him eye contact while she delivered the bad news. "We're going to die unless everyone gets out of the sim so the ship will let us go home."

The boy broke her gaze but didn't otherwise react. Hard to process anything when you were exhausted.

Kyle slapped the glass so that the boy jerked back. "They never understand. They think it'll be easy to get out again." Kyle crossed his arms, somehow looked authoritative even in his sweat-stained ship-issue uniform. Maybe he'd been captain of a sports team back at school and all uniforms were the same to him. He spoke at the glass. "You know anything about avalanches? Ever heard of people dying because they dig downward instead of toward the surface? They get tumbled around in the snow, get disoriented. That's how the sim is. Even when you know you're in a simulation, you end up losing your bearings and digging yourself in deeper."

Lake thought about how it had felt to wake from the sim not half an hour ago. That first gasp of breath, Willow's name on her parched lips. He wasn't wrong.

Lake pointed her algae shake at the prisoner watching from behind the glass. "I don't think he wants to go back into the sim. I think he's just thirsty." She moved the cup from side to side and the boy's gaze followed it. "I'll keep an eye on him, make sure he doesn't go anywhere."

Kyle crossed his arms again, considering. "Always out, never in," he said finally. That obnoxious motto again.

"Like burps and farts," Lake said with a smile.

Kyle looked more annoyed than amused.

But he didn't stop her when she went back to dragging the table.

The moment she cracked the door open, the boy behind it grabbed the cup from her.

He made a face at the taste. "Yeah, I know," Lake said apologetically.

He downed the rest and leaned heavily against the wall, exhausted. "Thanks," he croaked.

"How do you feel?"

"About right, for a dead person. I'm assuming this is hell."

"No . . ." Lake looked back, past the turmoil of the eatery, to the screens that showed Earth's distant surface. "That'd be what we left behind when we got on this ship." *Smoking craters and impact fires and blackened skies.*

"We left."

"The lucky ones did."

"And then . . . I was in a simulation?"

"You leave stasis, then you enter the sim before you fully wake up. It's supposed to show you what Earth's like now: war over, skies clear." She pointed at the distant view-screen he'd been staring at earlier, where white clouds still swirled. "But it didn't get everything right. The sim's broken. Like the rest of this ship."

"The ship's . . . ?" He couldn't seem to bring himself to finish the sentence. His hand shook so much Lake thought he might drop the cup. "What do you mean?"

"The ship was never meant to be an emergency bunker. It was supposed to be for exploration. You know the guy who made the virtual reality app Paracosm? He had this ship built so he could, like, *boldly go.* But I guess it wasn't quite finished when the war started and we all hurried aboard."

The boy's legs shook. They weren't used to holding him up. Lake thought about telling him to take a seat, that all the news she had was bad news anyway. But he was pressing up against the wall as if he were trying to get as far as possible from what she was saying.

"I was trapped in there, wasn't I?" he asked. "In the sim."

Lake gave him a sympathetic smile. "Now you're just trapped on the ship. Until everyone gets out of the simulation.

The ship won't let us leave until then. Won't let us access most of its areas, let alone the shuttles. We've got a whole group of volunteers trying to beat down the doors to the shuttle bay on a twenty-four-hour rotation. But I'm pretty sure those doors can withstand a lot more than homemade battering rams."

This was usually the point when the newly rescued went back to slumping. The boy just gave her a determined grimace. Fine, he could join battering-ram duty when he found his strength. She wouldn't stop him from wasting his time.

"How do we get people to wake up?" he asked.

Lake's shoulders stiffened. *A normal question,* she told herself. *It doesn't mean he knows it was you in the sim.* "We let them figure it out on their own."

He eyed her like he knew she was lying.

Lake ducked his gaze. She leaned forward and took the empty cup from his trembling hand before he could drop it, noted the stars tattooed on his forearm—some constellation. "What's your name?"

"Taren."

"Don't try to go back into the sim, Taren. Forgetting reality feels nice for a while, but in the end, it only makes you more miserable." *Trust me.*

He stared at her a long moment, and Lake couldn't decide whether he believed her. The new ones usually didn't. "What's *your* name?" he finally asked.

"Lake."

"Why did you look at me that way before, Lake? When you were eating at the table? No one else bothered to notice me."

Her skin itched. *He's going to figure it out. And then they'll put* me *in here.* "I have an eye for potential organ failure." She shrugged. "Just—don't go back into the sim. If anyone finds out, they'll lock you up for good."

She slipped back out the open door, dropped the cup on a table, and left the eatery, forcing herself to take it slow under the weight of his gaze.

3

LAKE

The sim was shrinking.

With every person who woke, a section of it closed for good.

So why was it still so full of empty pockets?

Lake wandered a neighborhood where the houses sat at drunken angles, their foundations cracked in soggy soil. Every door along the street stood open.

"Where did they go?" Lake wondered aloud.

She sat on the tilted porch of an empty house, her head in her hands. It was getting harder to find pockets of the sim she hadn't already searched. And the pockets she did find were lonely places, full of gloom and silence.

But there was one place she could go that she knew wouldn't be empty.

She got to her feet and turned toward the unfamiliar house whose porch she'd been moping on, wishing now with her whole heart that it was her own house. She closed the front door, waited a beat, opened it again.

It should have led her into a stranger's cobwebbed home. Instead, Lake stepped right through to the backyard, as if the front of the house were a movie-set façade.

Not just any backyard, either.

Her own. Patchy lawn, birch tree, and—

"Willow." Lake's breath went out of her.

There was Willow, kneeling in the middle of the yard, holding an ordinary garden spade like an ordinary person.

Her small, wiry frame was bent with determination. Brown hair mostly free from its ponytail, pointed chin smudged with dirt. Jacket hanging off one shoulder in that way she'd started wearing it.

But it's not really her. It's just the sim.

Lake stepped onto the grass, and it gave under her feet just like real grass. The jasmine along the back fence thickened the air with sweetness. Bees droned, unseen. In the shade of the birch tree, Willow smoothed a patch of dirt with her garden spade. She pushed messy hair away from her face, just like a real person would. The sun shone, birds whistled. So real.

Lake tried saying what a real sister would say: "I've been looking for you everywhere, dummy."

"Everywhere but the backyard of the house I live in?" Willow said, cracking a smile. "Who's the dummy, then?"

This isn't real. Willow's messy hair hanging like smoke around her face. Her bare feet glowing in the sunlight at the edge of the birch's shade.

"Mom's going to be mad that you were digging in her yard," Lake said.

"I buried something."

Back home, Willow always did stuff like that. Collected shells from the nearby beach and hid them in her drawer, found sticks in the garden and made fairy houses under the bushes. "That's not going to make Mom any happier."

"I like knowing there's a secret under the dirt," Willow said. "I like that there's something in the world that only I know about."

Lake held out her hand and helped Willow up, astonished that Willow's palm against hers was enough to tame the fierce loneliness she'd felt only moments before.

From her sister's wrist hung a blue bracelet of knotted thread, matching Lake's own. Strange, how something so insubstantial could keep them tethered to each other.

"Come on," Lake said. "If you're done burying treasure."

Willow tried to turn back to the house, thinking they were going inside. And the sim would have obliged her, if Lake wanted it to. It would re-create their home, right down to the scuff marks on the kitchen tile.

But Lake said, "Not in there. I can't . . ."

Willow gave her a questioning look.

"I can't go in there," Lake said. It was a vault she'd never get out of. "Let's use the gate."

She led Willow to the tall fence and lifted the latch on the gate.

"We're not going to the pier again, are we?" Willow asked. "It's creepy when there's no one else there. The carousel looks haunted—all those sun-bleached horses."

"No. I'm tired of empty places." Lake opened the gate, picturing the place she wanted to go next.

"I buried something," Willow said before Lake could steer her through.

"You said that already."

"I like that there's something in the world that only I—"

"Please, Will." Lake pressed her eyes closed, unnerved. "You're repeating yourself."

Willow sighed. "You think *everything* I do is annoying."

Lake tugged Willow's jacket back onto her shoulder. Willow slipped it right back off. Just like the real Willow would.

Lake's heart squeezed. *I shouldn't keep coming here.*

She took Willow's hand and turned to the gate. "Good thing I'd rather be annoyed by you than entertained by anyone else."

No more lonely neighborhoods, Lake decided. *Not today.*

So here was a pub. Scuffed doorway, high-backed wooden booths, dull copper walls. Muted piano music, as though someone were playing in a back room. Lake knew every note. Same tune every time she came.

Same boy at the bar, now adding to a ceiling-high model bridge made entirely of toothpicks. Ransom had a gift for making his corner of the sim ordinary and dreamlike at the same time.

Lake walked toward him, her worn boots hitting the wooden floor with a noise that made him turn on his stool. He leaned back against the bar, his shirt stretching over his chest, his body forming a long, sloping line. Lake breathed smoke that hadn't been there a moment ago, saw the gloom in his eyes veiled through it. She pressed herself against the bar next to him. "Good day or bad day?" she asked.

He intertwined his fingers with hers. The warmth of his palm melted some of her anxiety. "Want to guess?"

Lake looked over his toothpick bridge rising from bar to ceiling. A jagged mass of splinters. "That the Golden Gate?"

"Does it look golden." His voice dropped on the last word. He drew in a mouthful of the smoke hanging in the air and blew it back out.

Bad day.

"How about I buy you a drink?" Lake said.

He lifted her hand in his and kissed her knuckles. "Ah, but we're all out of ice. Not to mention glasses. And anything liquid." He nodded at the bottles lined up behind the bar, faintly wet but otherwise empty, rows of glass teeth.

Lake sank back from him. "Why are you punishing yourself?"

"Maybe I've got a limited imagination."

Pennies covered the pub's walls in careful rows, glinting through the tracery of smoke. Ransom's creation, along with the rest of the pub. "I'll never believe that." Lake trailed her fingers over his temple.

He pulled away from her touch, apparently unable to escape whichever particular brand of gloom had overcome him that day. Or no—something else was making him uneasy. Lake followed his gaze to where Willow sat in a booth like she was waiting for service, the green of her jacket muted by swirling smoke.

"Aren't you going to say hi to Willow?" Lake asked.

Ransom threw Lake a dark look and turned back to his toothpick bridge. "Why are you punishing yourself, Lake?"

Smoke in her lungs, in her stomach.

Ransom sighed. "Hi, Willow." He balanced a toothpick on a bridge strut. It quivered, then stuck, like a magnet to iron.

"He doesn't like me," Willow said to the smoke floating around her. She offered Ransom a catlike smile. "Is it because I'm thirteen and crashing your bar? Or is it the other thing?"

"There's no alcohol here," Ransom pointed out.

"So it's the other thing. The *not real* thing."

Lake tugged on Ransom's hand, desperate to redirect the conversation. "Don't be upset about Willow. I can only spend so much of my time in the sim by myself."

He traced his thumb over hers. "So don't spend so much time in the sim. You hang around fake people more than you do real people."

Lake got that feeling again: smoke churning in her stomach. "*Someone* has to clear the place out."

Ransom turned to work on his bridge, so Lake's view was only of his tensed back.

"Most of the pockets I find lately are empty," Lake said. "Any idea where everyone's gone?"

"They must be grouping together."

"You haven't seen anyone lately?"

Ransom shrugged. "Don't get around much."

Lake watched him add to his impressive sculpture. "Do you even try anymore?"

"I try." He rubbed a hand over his eyes. "I wind up in the

same few pockets. The beach where we met, a couple other places. The sim doesn't work right for me."

"And no one comes here."

"No one except you." He gave Willow a reluctant glance. "And her."

"What a nice bridge," Willow said, an edge to her voice. "Did you do the pennies, too?" She peered through the smoke at the pub's copper walls.

"You asked me that last time," Ransom said, taking another toothpick from a box on the bar.

"When was that?" Willow asked.

Ransom nudged the toothpick into place. "Hard to measure time here. Let's say, one bridge ago."

Willow stood and wandered closer to the bar. "Once at school they showed us a black-and-white photo of the Golden Gate Bridge. It was all jagged, hanging in the air on cables." She touched the splintered edge of the toothpick bridge, frowning as if in concern. "If you didn't know it was half-built, you'd think a monster had snapped it in half."

Ransom dropped his toothpick at the word *snapped*. "Don't break my bridge, Willow."

"I would never," Willow said flatly, her hand still lingering.

Ransom picked up the fallen toothpick, licked it so it'd stay in place, stuck it on a ladderlike bridge-tower. "It's all I have to show for my time in the sim."

"You met *me* in the sim," Lake reminded him.

Ransom smiled. "Guess the sim's not all bad, then."

Lake thought of the dappled shade the birch tree made in her simulated backyard. Thought of Willow kneeling in grass as if it were another ordinary day. *No, it's not all bad. That's what makes it so dangerous.* "The music's not the best," she said.

"You don't like my music?" Ransom said, and in the back room the piano playing stopped.

"Well. I like hearing what kind of music you listen to when no one's around."

"Sad shit, mostly." He cracked another smile. "Gets me in the mood for when company finally comes around."

She slipped her hands into his and pulled him closer, wishing she were one of his magnetic toothpicks and he were a toothpick bridge. "I wish I could come more often."

"I wish I could leave."

She dropped his hands. "That would be nice." She gestured toward the bridge. "Ever seen it in person?"

Ransom tipped his head to one side, neither a yes nor a no.

"I could help you if you would tell me things like that," Lake said. "If you would tell me anything about your life before."

"I don't like it when you do your trick on me," Ransom told Lake. "The thing you do to people who are stuck in the sim."

"The thing I do? You mean, help people get out?"

"You think you can figure me out and I'll suddenly be able to leave. But that would only help if my problem was remembering what's real and what's not." He looked at Willow, who stood now at the wall, trying in vain to dislodge a penny.

I remember Willow isn't real. How could I forget? "You won't let me help you because you're afraid I *can't*," Lake told him.

"I won't let you help me because I don't want you wasting more time in the sim than you have to."

Lake smiled sadly. "I don't believe you."

"You never do." He rested a hand on her shoulder. "Not when I tell you how dangerous the sim is, or when I tell you it's got a stronger grip on you than you think."

Lake pulled away from him, uneasy at the desperation in his voice. *He wants me to stay away from Willow. But how can I?*

"I know all of that," she said. "What I don't understand is how you can know the sim isn't real and still be trapped inside it. I don't understand why you can't move through it the same way I can, why you get stuck."

"I think I only go where Lake takes me in the sim," Willow cut in. "But I'm not sure. I have a hard time remembering."

Lake gave her a faint smile. "It's okay, Will."

"Maybe if someone else came with us in the sim," Willow said, "they'd be able to take us to another pocket?"

"I can't bring other people in," Lake said. "Too much of a chance they'll get stuck again."

"Speaking of," Ransom said. "How long have you been in today?"

"Kicking me out?"

"I don't think she even sleeps anymore," Willow said.

"I sleep," Lake said.

Ransom's face was lined with worry. "Sim-sleep doesn't count."

"I don't like the dreams I have after I've been in the sim. They feel wrong. Blue trees, a frozen sun. I think it's a side effect of using the sim."

That only seemed to agitate Ransom further. The box of toothpicks fell to the floor and scattered.

Ransom didn't bother picking them up. "I'm worried about you. I'm worried you're spending so much time in the sim that you're forgetting what's real."

"What's the sim good for, if not for pretending to have what you can't?" She pulled him close, ready to make that glum look vanish.

Then—

A thunder of boots from beyond the doorway.

Lake shot to her feet.

The way Taren looked at me in the eatery, like he knew.

Like he might tell someone.

"Someone knows I'm here."

"What're you talking about?" Ransom asked.

"The door, Ransom! Someone's here."

Ransom threw out a hand so that, across the pub, the door slammed shut through the sheer force of his will.

Then—a sound of thunder. Someone pounding on the door.

Lake backed along the bar, toward Willow. "Come on, Will, we have to go."

Confusion clouded Ransom's expression. "Lake, what's going on?"

"Can't you hear it?" Lake said. "Someone's pounding on the door!"

The blows against the door kept coming. The doorknob rattled loud as gunfire.

Lake had to shout. "The door to the back room?"

"There's no back room," Ransom said. "That door is the only way out." He looked between the door and Lake, still confused. But he moved to the end of the bar and grabbed a baseball bat propped there, ready to defend her.

"Forget the bat," Lake said. "There's got to be another way out." She gripped Willow's hand and pulled her around the bar to crouch on the sticky mat.

Hiding won't work. Her lungs hurt from breathing so fast.

She turned and found a row of cabinets behind her. "Ransom! I need something to mark the cabinet door!"

A cracking sound, and then Ransom appeared with a piece of bridge he'd wrenched free. Lake pointed to the only cabinet door big enough to let them crawl through, and Ransom fell to his knees to carve an X into it.

He jerked it open. "Go."

Lake hesitated. "What about you? It won't work for you."

"It'll take me to another part of the sim, at least."

Lake wrapped her hand around the back of his neck and pulled him into a kiss. "I'll find you later," she told him. Then she pushed Willow through the cabinet and crawled after her.

Woke up drenched in sweat.

Ransom's words rang in her head: *"You're spending so much time in the sim you're forgetting what's real."*

She wished she could believe that Willow had woken up somewhere on the ship too.

But that hadn't been Willow.

Just a figment.

"I miss you like crazy," Lake said to the empty stasis chamber.

She lifted the lid and tumbled out of the bed, bones weighted with loneliness. She almost couldn't bring herself to slide open the chamber's steel panel, because she knew it would feel terrible not to see Willow waiting on the other side.

I'll see her when I go back in, at least.

After a long moment, she tugged the handle and heard the click of the panel-door unlocking. It slid aside.

And there stood Taren.

Lake's heart hammered in her chest.

So it was true: he'd guessed her secret.

"Lake?" He'd been waiting for her. And if he told the others what he knew . . .

They would make sure she'd never go back into the sim again.

4

L A K E

"You followed me?" Lake spat, because what else was there to say. Taren knew her secret. It was all over.

Kyle and his gang would lock her up, and she'd never see Willow's face again.

Taren took a step back, as if the edge in Lake's voice might cut him. "I just wanted to know if you—"

"Are you going to tell them?" Lake broke in. "They'll lock me up like they did to you."

Taren gave her a searching look. "So you *were* the girl who got me out of the sim. I thought you might have been, when you looked at me that way in the eatery. But your clothes were different in the sim, your hair was darker." He scrutinized her face.

"My expression was less enraged?" Lake suggested.

Taren held up his hands, palms out. "I promise I'm not going to tell anyone. I only banged on the door because you were in there so long I thought something had gone wrong."

"You banged on the door?" Lake slid the steel panel partway closed. "This door?"

Taren nodded. "I didn't know how to get you out."

Lake studied him, piecing it together. She must have heard him pounding on the door to her stasis chamber while she was in the sim. Her brain had interpreted it as someone pounding on the door to the penny pub.

But she definitely didn't remember asking him to try to rescue her.

"I didn't look at you any kind of way in the eatery," she said. She was spiraling into a deep, bruising disappointment. How could she be sure he wouldn't tell anyone her secret?

"I saw your bracelet." His gaze went to Lake's hand still lingering on the door handle. "That's how I knew for sure."

Lake looked down at the blue knotted thread. She never changed it when she altered the rest of her appearance in the sim. She relied on the sight of it to keep her grounded in reality.

And anyway, she couldn't bear to see it look any different than it had when Willow had given it to her.

"You just pop in and out of the sim to help people get out?" Taren asked. "Like you're Trinity from *The Matrix*?"

"Lower your voice, *Neo*." Lake pulled him into the cramped space and slid the panel shut behind him. The lock clicked.

She sat on the bed while he stood crammed into the corner, gaping at the wires sprouting next to her.

"I told you, we're all stuck on this ship until everyone clears out of the sim," Lake said. "And the ship isn't exactly in great condition."

Taren pressed his hands into the wall behind him in a poor

attempt to steady himself. "What does that mean, exactly? Give me the whole Checklist of Doom this time. Promise I can take it."

"Even though you're shaking?"

He made an attempt to stand straighter, and then had to lean all his weight against the wall again. "Side effect of stasis."

"Anyway, I'm not a mechanic." Lake hesitated, but he seemed hungrier for bad news than any other sleeper she'd ever awakened. "The algae supply seems to be holding up okay, but I'm not as confident about breathable air."

"The CO_2 scrubbers are failing?"

"All I know is that when the light next to the word *oxygen* starts flashing red, that's generally bad."

He took a shaky breath. "Generally, yeah."

"Are you going to be sick?"

He shrugged off her question. "How long have we all been asleep?"

"Decades. No one really knows how many. Probably at least thirty years. The ship was supposed to wake us up when it had evidence that we'd be okay to go home to the surface. But it hasn't really been keeping to any other protocols so we're not sure about that one, either."

"Shit."

"Sorry. No one likes waking up to bad news."

His face suddenly looked sunken. Lake gently pulled him to sit on the edge of the stasis bed. The nodes that engaged the sim twitched and clicked just out of reach, like hungry fish snapping at bait.

"Where's the captain?" he asked.

"Dead, maybe," Lake said. "Never seen him in the sim anyway."

"I remember his lottery at school. They told us some billionaire had been building a private ship before the war even started, and he was going to pick one hundred and fifty students from five schools to come aboard. They wouldn't let you prove you deserved a spot—it was all going to be random." Taren skimmed his fingers over the head brace built into the bed. The metal arms contracted slightly, and he jerked his hand away. "The captain—he's that tech guy, right? The one who made the VR app? I remember him from the video they showed at school. Smug genius type, really pleased with how generous he was being."

"Seems like his ship wasn't exactly seaworthy when he loaded us onto it. But I guess that's the tech industry for you—push it out now and patch it later." She meant it as a joke, but the thought of the ship needing a patch it would never get was almost more than she could take at the moment.

"And there aren't *any* adults on board?" Taren asked.

"I guess he figured he'd leave the engineers and politicians to the government ships and bunkers."

"So we're on our own."

"Looks like it."

Taren shuddered, like he might be sick after all. The room filled with the sound of the head brace clicking, searching for something to latch on to.

Lake tried to think of something to say, to soften the blow of all the bad news. "I'm sorry—"

"I want to go back into the sim with you," Taren cut in. "Help you wake people up."

The new ones always try to go right back in. "It's not that easy."

"*You* do it."

Lake stood, touched the door handle.

"Wait." Taren put his hand on her arm. "We're going to die on this ship if we don't leave it soon. I don't much feel like waiting around for that. I did enough waiting in the sim."

Lake stared at the stars tattooed on his arm, avoiding his heated gaze. "You think that if you go back in, you'll remember you're in a simulation. You think you won't get stuck again. But you'll forget. The sim will make you forget that it's not real."

"*You* remember, when you go back in. You remember you're in a simulation."

Most of the time. "I've had a lot of practice."

Taren dropped his arm. His gaze roved the tiny chamber, lit on bundled wires snaking down the side of the bed. "What about your sister?"

Lake tensed.

"You told me in the sim that you were searching for her," Taren said. "Did you ever find her? I could help you look."

"My sister never got on board the ship."

"I thought younger siblings of lottery winners were supposed to be allowed to board."

"Until all the spots filled up. I had to leave her behind, and now she's gone." Her words dropped heavy as stones between them. "No bunker for her, or for my parents. No way any of them survived."

She expected him to reel at her words, but he only tilted his head in a sympathetic way. "None for mine, either," he said.

The overhead light flickered. Machinery hummed. Lake wished for Willow, alive and well and digging holes to hide treasures in.

"I don't go into the sim to search for my sister," she said. "I go because everyone on this ship got a spot my sister didn't. I'm not going to let them waste it."

Taren winced, then tried quickly to cover his reaction.

"Don't feel guilty," Lake said. "It's not like you're the specific person who took my sister's spot."

Taren studied the constellation of tattooed stars on his arm. "My brother got a spot on a government ship. He went up before I did. Mechanical engineer, conscripted from Lockheed."

"That's good."

"You want to know the worst thing I've ever seen? The video feed cutting out when his ship broke apart in space."

Now, Lake was the one left reeling.

Taren balled his fists on his knees. "Gray was a *mechanic*. He was supposed to make it. I'm not anything. If they had asked us to earn our spots on this ship, I don't think I could have."

"No one earned their salvation. Only the rich and lucky survived."

Taren pinned her with his gaze. "And luck runs out."

The overhead light flickered again, as if to prove his point.

"You can't tell me you don't need help in the sim," Taren said.

Lake couldn't deny it. It was like Willow had said—if Lake took Taren into the sim, he might find a pocket she couldn't.

Or he might get himself stuck again, after all my hard work getting him out.

"You don't know what you're asking to get yourself into." Lake turned the door handle and listened to the click of the lock releasing.

"Lake—"

"We can't go into the sim right now," she said over her shoulder. "We need to eat something, fuel up. There's a lot you have to learn before you can wake sleepers."

5

TAREN

The day Taren won a ticket off the smoldering Earth was the same day his brother left to claim a spot on a government ship. Taren's parents had been rigid with fear for days after reports of fallout and firestorms, but now they slumped like broken dolls, as if they knew they could give up on surviving because their sons would survive enough for all of them.

Then the reports had come: the government ship had broken apart in space during a fuel transfer to its correctional thrusters. Taren couldn't stop picturing it in his mind: the ship coming apart like a great hot egg bursting. Debris shooting out in all directions. Some of which had to have been people—the *remains* of people. Of his own brother. Sometimes when the images played in his head, Taren would hold his breath, as if that could stop the ship from breaking apart. As if it were a wish flower and he could keep the seeds from scattering.

Taren erased the thought now as he stepped into the stasis chamber, ignoring his stomach's complaints about the food he'd just given it. *That's all I have, there's not exactly a buffet on board.*

He tried not to feel cheated. He'd gone from a barren sim to a busted ship. From eating wild plants to drinking algae. Plus, no dog and no sunshine.

It didn't surprise him that those who left the sim usually wanted to go right back in.

But this wasn't about escaping reality. He wouldn't lose himself to the sim. Not with that image of destruction always looming at the edge of his mind. His brother had earned the right to survive—and hadn't gotten his due. Taren had only ever been lucky.

And like he'd told Lake, luck runs out.

"You okay?" Lake asked, leaning in the doorway of the stasis chamber. "If you're not up for this—"

"I'm up for it." He hadn't downed more liquid algae for nothing. "Are you, though? You look like you haven't slept in months."

She rubbed a hand over her lined face. "Using the sim gives me weird dreams."

"Nightmares?" He'd had his fair share of those.

"I have this recurring dream where I'm stuck in a place between night and day. Blue and purple trees, everything in twilight."

"Doesn't sound bad."

"Sometimes I'm being chased."

"Oh." He looked down at the bed and was suddenly eager to change the subject. "How do I do this?"

Lake glanced in at the nest of bundled wires and nodes and

metal brackets. "It knows what you want. Just crawl in and relax. Pretend it's a slumber party."

"But how does it—"

"Not a mechanic, remember?"

She doesn't actually know how it works.

He imagined the plastic shell lowering over the bed, shutting him into a high-tech coffin. And then he would have to just lie there and hope everything worked the way it was supposed to.

He forced himself to sit on the bed. "Is this the kind of slumber party where we tell ghost stories first?" he joked.

"I'm not much for ghosts anymore, are you?"

Taren pictured a hot egg bursting in space, the particles drifting forever. "Not so much."

He still couldn't bring himself to lie down. Lake must have sensed it because she pushed on his chest enough to convince his weak body to go horizontal.

"You know the tiled steps at Sixteenth Avenue?" she asked. "That's where we'll meet up in the sim. Just picture it and you should end up there."

"Just . . . picture it? Are you sure that's going to work?"

Lake stood outside the doorway and reached around for the door handle, ready to shut the panel for him. "I'll be in the next chamber over."

Taren wanted to nod, but something cold and metallic pressed against the sides of his head.

Don't get trapped, he told himself. *This ship isn't going to last much longer.*

A click at Taren's temples cut off his thoughts.

Only darkness for a moment, and then letters flickered across his vision:

PARACOSM: THE WORLD WE CREATE TOGETHER

Everyone used Paracosm back home—for VR-calls and gaming and homework and shopping. It wasn't surprising that the billionaire genius who'd invented it had also put it on his own ship. It was only surprising that, here on the ship, it didn't seem to work so great.

The letters vanished, and then Taren was surfacing from a dream instead of descending into one. A fog of vagueness, the sleepy ritual of digging his fingers into his hair. He realized with a jolt that the bed was no longer underneath him. He had a sudden sense that he was falling—but no, he was standing. Feet firmly on the ground.

The scene before him sharpened into focus: a tall staircase leading up a steep hillside, its steps embedded with blue and white tiles that gave the impression of swirling ocean currents. For a moment, Taren's reality swirled just as strangely, and then a hand gripped his elbow, anchoring him.

"We're not going up," Lake said. "This is just a spot for us to meet up. Come on."

She steered him from the steps. When they turned, Taren discovered a row of crumbling houses, a neighborhood sinking into a thicket of weeds.

"I've been to this pocket before," Lake said. "Empty—no sleepers."

Taren peered at the row of houses: railed balconies and

shuttered windows. He recognized this neighborhood. Except now, the balconies tilted and the windows held no glass.

"My house isn't far from here," he said. He spotted a pale shape in the grass at the end of the street—his dog, waiting for him. "That's my dog. Or anyway, it's the dog I found wandering the streets."

"That's not your dog," Lake said. "None of this is real."

"He's right there. Just give me a minute to tell him I'm sorry I left him behind."

"A minute to let you forget you're in the sim." Lake gestured at the houses. "None of these houses are real. Someone was feeling sorry for themselves and re-created this place so they could pretend they were home."

Taren squinted at the pale spot in the distance. "That's not my dog?"

"We're going to move on, okay? We can't stay here." Lake pulled him to the door of the nearest house, opened it, and led him through . . .

Into a pub where hundreds of pennies glinted on the walls. "Where are we?"

Lake walked along a line of wooden booths. "Just checking on someone."

A metallic sound rang through the place. On the bar, the ruins of a toothpick sculpture made the shape of a toothy jaw. Next to it, a coin spun, as though someone had only just left the room. "What . . . ?" It went on spinning, impossibly.

I'm in a simulation.

His head hurt.

Lake was watching him, frowning with concern. Taren did

his best to shake off his confusion. He straightened his back. Man, it felt good not to have the post-stasis shakes.

He looked over the empty booths. "No one's here."

"But he was." Lake watched the coin spin on the bar. "Recently."

"Who?"

"Never mind. I'll find him later. I just like to make sure he's okay." She turned back to the door. "The first thing we need to do is go someplace where you can change your appearance. If anyone recognizes you in the sim, they'll give you trouble later on the ship."

Taren tore his gaze from the coin still spinning on the bar. "Change my appearance? How am I supposed to do that?"

"Try hard." At his look, Lake blew out a breath. "The simulation is just like the Paracosm app back home. Just tell it how you want things to look. Or think it."

"So I just, like . . . ask for a hat? Right here and now?"

"I wouldn't recommend a hat for you," she said, squinting at him. "And you can only change things in areas of the sim you've created yourself."

"But I haven't created any . . ." Taren thought of the tiger yard he'd spent the last few months in. His own empty fortress. "The zoo—I created that?"

"Most people stick to houses," Lake said. "And other places fit for humans."

Taren's face heated. "I told you, I went to my house first. But nothing felt right there. I opened the back door and . . ." *It doesn't make any sense.* ". . . instead of my backyard, it was only a huge crater, like a bomb had fallen right there and hadn't even toppled my house."

"That's sim-logic for you."

"But you're saying I created my own house in the sim?"

Lake nodded.

"And I put in a crater in the backyard?"

"If it helps, you're not the only one who can't get over what happened after we left the surface."

"And after I left my house, I must have wanted to go someplace I'd feel safer."

"You feel safe in a zoo?"

"Whenever I'd go to that zoo as a kid, I would get obsessed with the idea that nobody ever messes with the tiger."

"The sim can only do so much—pretty sure it can't change you into a tiger."

Taren grinned. "That'd be cool, though, right?"

"Okay, sure." Lake sighed. "But the sim-zoo you were living in is gone now. When you leave the sim, any pocket you created closes. Which is half the reason we're doing this. The more pockets we close, the less strain the sim puts on the ship's failing systems."

"But you want me to create a new pocket?"

"A small one, yeah. It'll close when we leave the sim."

Taren took a deep breath, thinking. "So, should I create my house again?"

Lake shook her head. "Never go into your own house if you can help it, or into any place that makes you feel like you won't want to get back out again. Pick something else."

She opened the pub door. Beyond was flat darkness, like a perfectly smooth curtain. "Think of what should show up on the other side of the door. Say it out loud if you want. Choose some place you've been in the real world. Nothing too inviting, just a place you've been to enough times to remember some details. School, maybe—no one tends to stay there long."

"That'd be kind of a waste after an apocalypse did me the favor of flattening it." Taren pictured another place instead, somewhere in his neighborhood, because that felt easiest to do at the moment. He stepped through the door . . .

Into a tiny convenience store crowded with shelves of packaged food. Smell of a/c coolant, *ding* of electronic door-chime.

Lake came through after him and stood there a moment surveying the shelves.

"The sim got all of this from my brain?" Taren asked.

"Yeah." Lake stepped closer to a rack of chips. "This is what you miss from Earth?" She held up a bag of chips identical to every other bag on the rack before her. "Flaming Hot Cheetos?"

Taren slowly pivoted to take in rack after rack of red chip bags. Months of eating dandelion leaves and the bitter roots of strange woody plants, and then waking up to a breakfast of yet more plants, this time blended into goo, so shockingly unfair. And now this—the same food he'd once eaten while playing video games and agonizing over trig homework and taking winding car rides to Santa Cruz.

Bags and bags of it. "Damn."

"He's impressed with himself," Lake said to the bag in her hand. "I bet he dunks them in Mountain Dew."

"Sour cream, actually." His mouth was starting to water. "Mountain Dew is for Doritos."

Lake made a face. "Boys are weird."

Taren took a few steps farther into the store. A teenage guy behind the counter, thumbing through a magazine, announced, "We've got mirrors," and pointed at the huge security mirrors angled in the ceiling corners.

"Who's he?" Taren asked, startled enough that the sleepy vagueness finally cleared from his head.

"Figment of the sim," Lake said. "Like an NPC in a video game. Non-player character. He's just here to set the scene."

Taren turned to watch the guy behind the counter swipe aside a magazine page. "We've got mirrors," he said again, and pointed the same way he had before.

Lake pulled Taren back from the counter. "Just focus on changing your appearance. Consider this your chance to try whatever facial hair you couldn't manage back home."

"Would it weird you out if I tried a neck tattoo?"

"Absolutely."

Taren lifted a magazine from a rack near the counter. "Fine. I'll just go blond." He focused on the face on the magazine while he moved his jaw, trying to widen it. Scrunched his brow, bugged his eyes. "Is this working or am I just embarrassing myself?" He looked up at an angled mirror and saw an unfamiliar face staring back at him.

"Hey, genius," Lake said, "you don't think people are going to notice that you look exactly like their favorite movie star?"

Taren smiled sheepishly. "Okay, sorry." He rubbed his hands through his hair and the strands shrank. "Better?"

Lake glanced at the tattoo on his right forearm, and Taren tensed at the thought that she might ask him to change it. But all she said was, "Is that a constellation?"

"Taurus," he said tightly. "My brother Gray and I were both born in May."

She nodded, toying with her thread bracelet. Then she turned her attention to the shelves and poked a bag of Cheetos. "Chip up and let's get out of here. This is just a pit stop."

Taren seized handfuls of chip bags. Anything to get the taste of algae out of his mouth. You'd think that would go away once you'd escaped into a simulation. He glanced at the guy behind the counter. *Can a figment stop people from shoplifting?*

I just want one normal thing. Taren was ready to explain it to him if he had to. *Just one normal thing before I have to wake up in the closet of a spaceship.*

"He's not going to bust you—I think he only has the one line," Lake said. "Can you carry all those?"

The plastic rustled in Taren's grip, and he suddenly realized how pathetic he must look to her. All he could think of to say was "I haven't had Cheetos in . . ."

No way for either of them to know how to finish that sentence.

"You still haven't," Lake said with a glum smile.

Taren's head hurt again.

"Let's get out of here, okay?" Lake said. "Find some sleepers to wake."

"Where to?"

Lake scratched the back of her neck. "Good question. I was hoping you might have an idea." She flashed him a smile.

"Um, what?"

"There are fifty-two sleepers left in the sim, and probably twice as many pockets. Lots of people seem to be moving on from the pockets they've created and heading somewhere together. But I don't know where. And I keep ending up in pockets I've already visited."

He gaped at her. "You want me to find a corner of the sim you *haven't* found?"

"New person, new pockets—sounds like it could work, right?" She didn't wait for him to answer, just steered him back toward the door. "Clear your mind when you step through the door and see where it'll take you."

"Okay . . ."

Just clear my mind. So easy.

He stepped through the door . . .

Into a convenience store with racks of Cheetos.

"We've got mirrors."

Taren and Lake turned to look at the guy behind the counter. He swiped aside a page in his magazine.

"What . . . ?" Taren pushed his fingertips over his forehead. His bags of Cheetos lay at his feet. He didn't even remember dropping them.

"Didn't get enough Cheetos the first time around?" Lake said lightly. She leaned down to retrieve a bag and handed it to him. "You do remember where you are? Where you *really* are?"

Taren turned and stared at the red Cheetos bags on the rack under the counter. Turned back and stared at the red bags lining the aisles like rows of inflated tongues. "The sim."

"A-plus. So when you step through that door, there are about a hundred places you could wind up. Ninety-nine, if you don't want to wind up back in this convenience store."

"That isn't making this any easier."

"If you want, try thinking of a specific place. The sim is like a dollhouse, but for a city. Each room is a pocket of San Francisco—because that's the city everyone on the ship is from. Don't create a new pocket—just let yourself walk into one that's already there."

"Walk into a specific place," Taren echoed.

"Hey." Lake nudged his shoulder. "Just think of someplace. Where do you want to go?"

Her stare drilled into him. He stared back. "I want to go home. To my parents and my living room and the burger place near school where I hang out with my friends. And to my stupid kitchen, because I swear even though the sim takes away the feeling that my muscles have melted out of my body, it's somehow still registering that I'm absolutely starving."

Lake waited patiently, as if he might make a decision now that he'd gotten all that out.

"Where I want to go doesn't exist anymore," he said with a sigh. "Simulations don't count."

Lake didn't argue.

He respected that.

"Maybe this was a bad idea," Lake said. "It might be too much for someone who only just left the sim."

"No, it's not." Taren winced. "It's just—all of this is gone, isn't it? None of it exists on Earth anymore." He gestured to the museum of Cheetos.

"Convenience stores? No, probably not."

"I mean, *everything*. Places, people. We don't even know how many are left alive back home. They've been sitting in bunkers and shelters and ash-covered houses working to survive while we've been sleeping. All because some guy decided to let us on his ship."

Lake put a hand on his arm, the first reassuring touch he'd felt in decades. "Are you telling me these Flaming Hot Cheetos are just punishment for your sin of surviving? Because that makes a lot more sense."

He couldn't help cracking a smile. But it didn't last long. "Am I going to get off this ship?"

Lake held up a bag of Cheetos. "You sure you *want* to?"

Some of the tension in his chest eased. He batted the chips out of her hand, pretending to be annoyed at her joke.

"Ready now?" Lake held out her hand and nodded toward the door.

I have to get off this ship. Taren took her hand, opened the door, and stepped through.

6

TAREN

The crunch of underfoot snacks gave way to the squelch of wet gravel. The door had led them to a wooded hillside. A road cut through trees and widened into a driveway in front of a house that was all acute angles and vast plates of glass, like a chapel to wealth.

"Where are we?" Lake asked.

"I think I came here to do a homework project once with someone from my school," Taren said.

Lake turned, and then Taren did, following her gaze. A garden shed sat at the edge of the gravel drive, its shadowed doorway like a portal into the creeping fog.

"Is that the door we came through?" Taren asked.

"Yeah," Lake said. "I'll be right back."

"Wait, what?" Taren sputtered. "Where are you going?"

"Somewhere I can change my appearance," she said over her shoulder. "Sit tight."

"You don't think I should come with—"

The shed door opened with a squeal and then Lake was gone.

But she hadn't marked the door with an X, like when she'd taken him from the sim. She wasn't *leaving*.

He watched the shed door a little longer, doing his best to squelch his anxiety. Then he found a distraction in a bright spot among the gravel: a golden poppy. He leaned down to get a better look. How did the sim know how to make something like this? The buttery orange color, so rare you could use the petals for currency.

And the smell in the air—wet trees and earth. He could live off it if all food ran out.

Will it all be waiting for us when we get back?

Or is the world just a burnt shell of what it used to be?

The shed door shrieked.

A stranger stepped out. Taren skittered back, startled. Then he realized the stranger must be Lake. Her expression held the same hardness he'd become familiar with, but her face was different—wider, and framed by darker hair.

Same glint of anxiety in her eyes.

A girl had stepped through after Lake, maybe thirteen, following Lake like a compass follows north.

"Who's *this*?" Taren asked.

"This is my sister, Willow," Lake said. "She likes trees and cool houses. She's coming along."

The girl followed Lake uncertainly, her awkward steps scattering gravel.

"Wait," Taren said, gravel sliding under his feet as he hurried to catch up. "I thought you said your sister—" He broke off and threw an uncertain look at Willow.

"I think I only go where Lake takes me in the sim," Willow said. "But I'm not sure. I have a hard time remembering."

"What?"

Lake stopped and turned back to give Taren a cool look. "This is how I stay grounded in the sim. I know Willow isn't—" She broke off at the sound of Willow's nervous feet shuffling in the gravel. "If she's here with me, I know none of this is real."

Taren looked away from Lake's wounded gaze and studied her sister instead. Willow's green eyes were startling against the fog and muted moss. Hair messy, chin smudged with dirt. None of it was real? She was just part of the computer program?

And having her around was supposed to make Lake *more* likely to be able to leave the sim?

"Is this really a good idea?" he asked.

"Are Flaming Hot Cheetos really the best thing for your stomach lining?" Lake said, and turned back to the house.

"Okay . . . Guess we're not going to talk about this."

Willow hung back. "Like those espresso shots she buys after school are any better," she muttered to Taren.

Taren could only stare. *She's not real, and she's talking to me.*

"Are you coming?" Lake barked, and Willow hurried to catch up.

Taren followed more slowly, still unsure.

Lake pulled open the massive glass front door set into the wood paneling. "After you."

Taren swallowed his nerves. Inside the house, potted bamboo made graceful lines against reclaimed hardwood. Past the entryway, muted light filled tall windows in a sprawling living room, where half a dozen kids Taren's age lounged on a sky-blue couch and stood at the wet bar in the corner.

Taren gave Lake a triumphant smile. "You wanted to find someone to wake up."

"Don't look so smug." Lake stepped into the house after him and peered in at the scene. "It's harder when they're not alone." But Taren read the relief on her face—he'd found at least one of the pockets that had eluded her.

"You want me to distract them while you do your thing?" he asked her.

"My thing?"

"Carve an X in the door, lure them to an algae brunch."

"I told you, it's not that easy."

Taren noted a guy slumped on the couch, and another pouring a drink in the corner. Did she think they'd put up a fight? "You haven't seen my reach."

"Wow," Willow said, leaning in the doorway with her arms crossed. "Are you always like this at parties?"

Lake caught Taren's arm, claiming all his attention. "You can't throw people through a door to get them out of the sim. The X isn't magical. Whoever opens a door in the sim chooses where it leads next, and the X helps me envision that the door leads out of the sim. But even so, if a person isn't prepared to leave the sim, that door won't take them out of it.

None of these people are going to wake from this nightmare when they walk through a door unless they have a sense that they're leaving this reality for another, however small that sense might be."

Taren thought of when he'd left his camp in the tiger yard with Lake. The tin in his fist, a rock in his stomach. He hadn't understood where he was going, but he'd known he'd never come back.

"Before I left the sim, we talked about those cough drops I'd been saving." He shifted his gaze to the entryway wall, because it was a little embarrassing to talk about something as pathetic as eating old medicine. "I was holding the tin when I walked out the door. Was that part of the reason I managed to get out of the sim?"

"When I'm trying to wake a sleeper"—Lake gestured to the teens lounging in the next room—"I look for an object nearby that shows how they feel about leaving the sim, what they're hung up on. There's always something. The sim reflects what's on our minds."

Taren looked at the family photos hanging on the wall without really seeing them. "Is that how it works? You have to find an object, draw an X on the door—"

"None of this is magic," Lake cut in. "It's just what I've figured out works for me."

Taren summed it up: "A lot of talking, no fighting."

"If you can manage that," Lake said. "But take it slow—"

A girl perched on the back of the couch called out, "Oh, wow, *Taren*? Is that *Taren*?"

Wait, he knew this girl? He ventured closer and it hit him.

"We had a class together. Greek mythology?" He thought her name might be Sharon.

"Why are you lurking over there?" she said. "I thought you were some guy delivering food or something. Come join us."

Now he could see what they were watching on TV: a satellite image of Earth, its surface marbled with red and black. "What is that?" he asked.

"Firestorms. Impact clouds. You want a glass so you can toast with us?"

Taren took the glass she pressed into his hand, though he had gone so numb all over that he was sure he'd drop it.

A boy at the other end of the couch raised his own glass, but Sharon broke in with, "Don't say, *To cannibalism,* or something stupid like that. There are so many other things that make the end of the world interesting."

Taren glanced at Lake. She was studying the family photos hanging on the wall as if she were browsing a museum on a Saturday afternoon. *Okay, weird.* She didn't seem in a rush.

"To mutually assured destruction," the boy at the end of the couch said, raising his glass in a toast.

Sharon rolled her eyes. "That's so *Cold War.* What are you, eighty years old?" She turned to Taren. "Got anything better?"

Roiling clouds on the TV screen now, almost pretty. "To black rain." He lifted his glass, realized it was empty and so was hers. She pretended to drink and then laughed, her bright face framed by the smoke showing on the giant screen behind her.

This is crazy. "Sharon," he said, and hoped that was really her name. No protests from her, so he plowed on. "There's something I need to explain to you."

She lifted her eyebrows, waiting for a punch line.

"This is going to be hard for you to understand," he went on, "but you've probably had this feeling, right? That something strange is going on here?"

Her brows lowered. "You mean, because the world has gone to shit and I'm partying in some richie's house? Yeah, Taren." She took another drink from her empty glass.

Taren heard Lake walking up behind him. "Taren, wait."

But he could do this. "I'm trying to tell you." He watched her swirl imaginary ice around her glass. "This isn't real. You're not here. Remember the lottery at school? Remember winning a place on a ship? That's where you are, where you *really* are."

"What?" The glass slipped from her hand and tumbled onto the couch. Taren thought she might faint.

"Taren," Lake said, firmer this time. She grabbed his arm and pulled him back. It took him a moment to realize why: something black was oozing up from between the expensive floorboards, inches from where his foot had been.

"What is that?" he gasped.

"Don't touch it," Lake said.

She didn't need to tell him. Something about the way it oozed, the way it swallowed any light that touched it, the way it pushed a sound deep into his brain, like bones grinding—

"Back up," Lake said to Sharon, and the girl scrambled over the back of the couch. "Don't let anyone go near it."

Taren couldn't stop staring at the black stuff. "I did that, didn't I?" A sour taste filled his mouth. "How did I do that?"

Lake pulled Taren back farther, toward the door, where

Willow waited. "That tar appears whenever there's an incongruity," Lake explained. "Like when someone believes they're both at a party and *not* at a party."

"I don't understand."

"You can't just tell someone they're in a simulation," Lake said, dropping her voice low. "It's too jarring. It breaks their brain, and it breaks the program. Get it now?"

Taren tried not to resent the frustration in her voice. "You could have told me all that earlier."

From the doorway, Willow asked, "You forgot to give him the manual?"

Lake looked between Willow and Taren, eyes hard with annoyance. "I've never taught anyone this stuff before."

"If you touch the tar," Willow told Taren, "it'll knock you out of the simulation."

"Is that bad?" Taren asked.

"It sends your body into shock," Lake said. "Sometimes kills you."

"Sometimes."

Lake stared at him.

"I mean, as long as we're holding class here, what's *sometimes*?" Taren asked. "One in one hundred? One in ten?"

Willow said, "Are you a math guy?" Smiled like it was some great joke. "Do geometry next."

Taren frowned at her. "I thought figments were supposed to repeat the same couple of lines over and over. Maybe you should try that."

"Some of us are a little more advanced than that," Willow said with a snort. "Haven't you heard of *machine learning*?"

"The more figments interact with people, the more complex they get?" Taren glanced at Lake. "Guess that means you two have interacted a lot." *Why does that make me nervous?*

Lake shrugged, didn't meet his gaze. "Can you just remember that it takes time to wake people from the sim? You can't just walk up and make an announcement about the emergency exits."

"And if they don't *want* to leave the sim?" Taren asked. "What do you do then?"

Lake toyed with the thread-bracelet on her wrist. "I try again later."

And if they still *don't want to leave?*

But Taren decided to drop it. "So what now? We talk to them one by one?" He held his hands up in surrender. *"Slowly."*

"No. We don't need to wake them one by one." Her gaze went to the photos hanging on the wall. "If we can figure out whose house this is, we can wake just that one person. Whoever lives here most likely created this pocket of the sim. We wake them up, the pocket closes—gently, like a dream ending. All the other sleepers in the house wake up on the ship."

Taren blew out a sharp breath. "Another thing you could have told me sooner."

"I didn't realize you were a jump-right-in kind of guy." Lake pointed at one of the photos. "You see her anywhere? I'm pretty sure she's the dreamer we're looking for, the one who made this place."

Taren studied the face—brown eyes, freckles, a smile that could convince you only sunshine had ever fallen on the Earth. "She's not over there with the rest of them."

"Maybe she's out there," Willow said from the window. She pointed.

Lake went to look closer. "Ah, shit."

"What?" Taren asked, craning to see. In the distance, he spotted a metal door angled up from the ground.

"I think she's in a bunker," Lake said.

"And you don't think she'll let us in?"

"Believe it or not, getting in isn't the biggest problem. They're usually not even locked."

Willow's breath fogged the window glass. "Never go into your own house, or into any place that makes you feel like you won't want to get back out again."

"Like a bunker," Taren said.

Willow beamed. "He's learning."

"So we're back to waking them one by one," Taren said.

Lake eyed the tar oozing over the floor of the other room. "If we try that and we can't wake them all, we leave them here with the tar."

"And risk sending them into shock if they touch it," Taren said.

"Yeah." Lake squinted out at the metal door as if she were assessing a target.

"So we go down into the bunker together," Taren said, "and we remind each other that we're still in the sim. Isn't that why you brought me into the sim with you? To help?"

Lake crossed to the doorway and stood half in the wet air and tree-smell that Taren still couldn't believe was simulated. "No, *I* go down there to wake the dreamer, you stay up top. If you think I've been down too long, you come and get me out."

"You want to go down there alone?"

"Willow's coming with me."

Even worse. "I'll give you fifteen minutes."

Lake and Willow were already walking out the door.

7

HAILEY

Hailey had no way of knowing how long she'd been in the bunker. No signal—cell, Wi-Fi, radio. Ironic, because her dad used to tease her by saying she would die if she ever had to go without any of those things, and here she was, still practicing the fine arts of breathing and eating. When she'd first closed herself in, she'd started the clock that was supposed to count down to when it'd be safe to leave, but it only ever showed 076734, which, if you turned it upside down, spelled *hello*. A joke her dad had programmed in? She kept the door unlocked for whenever he might join her. He must have gone to find people who didn't have a place to shelter. She'd told him that they should do that, back when they'd first heard the bad news. At the time, she'd felt like she wouldn't need the bunker—she'd felt she'd be leaving for somewhere else. Now she couldn't remember why she'd thought that, but she was happy Dad wanted to help people.

She spent a lot of time re-watching historical dramas about

people living safely in the past, people who would never even *hear* the phrase *nuclear winter*. She would eat cereal on the leather lounge chair, feeling sorry for herself and telling the people on-screen, "You have no idea. *No* idea." Sometimes she'd watch this one old movie about the end of Mayan civilization, with its stark images and dramatic solar eclipse, and say, "*You* know what it feels like." She had one can of ravioli left and then it would be only gluey pea soup from there on out—the end of civilization.

Even so, it didn't really surprise her when the inner door of her bunker gave a squeal that meant someone was cranking the wheel to open it. It *annoyed* her, maybe, because she was trying to play Mario Kart, but it didn't *surprise* her when the door opened and two girls walked in. They weren't the first to have entered her bunker and she already knew what they wanted—the same thing the others had wanted: to take her to the Battery.

First thing the younger stranger said: "Is that Mario Kart?" As breathlessly as if she'd walked in on Hailey feasting on freshly delivered pizza.

The older one seemed to be mentally cataloging everything in the bunker: low leather furniture and pendant lights and floor-to-ceiling LED screens pretending to be windows showing views of sunny bluffs.

"I know," Hailey said, looking around at the décor her dad had once called *luxury apocalypse*. "Overkill."

The older girl stopped gawking and said, "The door was unlocked. Hope you don't mind."

"I'm guessing you didn't come to play Mario Kart." Hailey muted the game and stood, glad she'd changed out of her pj's today. "I've been spreadsheeting high scores for different vehicles—light karts, medium, heavy."

The older girl had a hollow stare, like maybe she hadn't spent the apocalypse watching Victorian dramas. Or eating ravioli. Or eating much at all.

"I think the medium-weight karts are edging out the others," Hailey added, offering an uncertain smile.

The girl nodded. Probably didn't have much to say about video games at this strange point in history. "Must be lonely down here."

Was that her way of asking if Hailey was alone? "You'd be surprised—I get visitors. They never stay, though. Other bunkers to visit, I guess." She smiled at her own joke, but the girl didn't seem to get it.

"You're lucky to have a bunker," she said.

"My dad had this built before the war even started," Hailey explained. "Not that he expected nuclear apocalypse. Lots of people in San Francisco were worried about class warfare, so they built bunkers or bought real estate in New Zealand or on Canadian islands. Naturally they spent their money on bunkers instead of on preventing the class warfare." She squirmed. *I'm wearing designer slippers.* It was all so stupid.

"Good news," the younger girl said. "No class warfare out there."

Hailey smiled at her. "Just nuclear fallout?"

The older girl pointed at the wall. "What happened there?"

Hailey's face heated. Between two LED window-screens, a spiderweb of cracks showed where she had bashed a chair against the wall. Something black and sticky oozed from the cracks. When Hailey looked at it, she felt her brain cells grind against one another.

"Bunker fever?" Hailey gave a nervous laugh. *Ugh, I sound like I'm losing it.* "You ever feel like you're stuck in a bad dream?"

The older girl took a deep breath. "Lately, yeah." She couldn't seem to pull her gaze from the busted wall.

"I don't hulk out or anything." Nervous laugh again. *Did the girl maybe just take a step back from me?* "It's just that I get confused and think there's something on the other side of the wall. And by something I don't mean, like, homicidal dirt monsters or anything. I just mean . . . trees and stuff."

The girl's gaze zoomed to Hailey. "Trees?"

Hailey laughed again, hoping they were sharing the joke now. "Trees with blue and purple leaves that the sun shines right through. Maybe I saw it in a movie and it got stuck in my head."

The girl toyed with a thread tied around her wrist. "Yeah. Maybe." Her brow furrowed. "I think I've seen the same movie."

The younger girl crept closer to the wall, marveling at the damage. "Should the walls of a bunker crack like that?"

"Willow, stay away from there." The older girl lurched to grab the younger girl's arm and pull her back.

"There's something bad about that black stuff," Hailey agreed. "She can look around the rest of the place if she wants. This is the only gooey corner."

The younger girl darted to the ladder that led to the sleeping nook.

"Don't break anything," the older girl called, and Hailey

almost laughed, because *the wall*. The older girl looked around the bunker again—but this time she seemed less interested in the furniture and more like she was searching for something. Her gaze stopped on a row of flowerpots under UV lights. "What happened to your plants?"

Hailey grimaced at the withered stalks. "They died. Guess I'm not going to be a farmer in the new world."

The girl moved to the pot at the end of the row. "Not *all* of them died. See?"

A single golden poppy showed bright against the potting soil.

"I think it's against the law to let state poppies die," Hailey said with a smile.

"It belongs outside. Don't you think? It's a wildflower."

Outside. Wind and rain and rustling leaves. "Is anything growing out there?"

"Come find out." The girl lifted the pot and held it out to Hailey like a gift.

Hailey's heart lifted with it. "I've been thinking of leaving. I packed a bag, actually." She pointed to her backpack near the door. "I didn't know if it was safe but the others said I should go with them. They said everyone's going to a place called the Battery."

The girl's arm dipped. The poppy trembled in its pot. "The Battery? Where's that?"

"They tried to explain how to get there. I *think* I can find it."

The flowerpot tipped as the girl turned to look at the backpack. "Maybe . . ." She seemed to remember she was holding what was possibly the last poppy in existence—was it?—and righted the flowerpot. Slowly, as if she were giving up a puppy, she lowered the pot back to its place under the UV lamp. "Can we come with you?"

The younger girl peeked out from the sleeping nook. "I found an Oreo."

Hailey winced. *I was saving that.*

"Come down, Willow," the older girl called. "We're going somewhere."

"Where?"

Wait, did I say they could come along?

But why not? It might even be nice not to go alone. The three of them could keep one another company, fight off apocalypse zombies together. *Please don't let there be apocalypse zombies.*

She forced a smile as the younger girl climbed down the ladder. *Why does something feel off?*

Then she thought of something the others had told her, something about a girl with a younger sister . . .

"Is she your sister?" Hailey asked, gesturing toward the ladder.

The older girl frowned.

Hailey remembered now the warning the others had given her. *She shows up and people disappear,* they'd said. *She and her sister—watch out for them.*

Hailey's mouth went dry. She forced another smile. "Your little sister probably hasn't gotten to do anything normal in a while, has she?" Her heart thumped. *Will this work?*

The younger girl had picked up a game controller and now turned to give her sister a pleading look. "One race? You owe me a rematch from when you broke our truce with a blue shell."

The older girl looked back at the door. "Don't you want to get going?"

Hailey shrugged. "Yeah, but who knows if this Battery place has Mario Kart. Could be our last chance to test my theory about medium-weight carts having an edge."

From the couch, the younger girl called, "Do you have any more food? She never eats anything, and it makes her miserable to be around."

"Willow," the older girl said tightly.

Hailey responded with her most pitying smile. "She's had it hard, hasn't she?" she said to the older girl. "You both have. You want to sit a minute? Bet there's no filtered air aboveground. Just hang out while I get the rest of my stuff, and then we can all leave together."

The older girl hesitated. She squinted at the door like she couldn't remember why she should be in a hurry to leave.

"You're lucky you two have each other," Hailey said, and this time she wasn't trying to bluff. Life in her bunker would be so different if she had someone to eat cereal with and compare kart stats and complain about pea soup. "I bet you haven't been apart since the day this all started."

The girl turned and looked at her sister lounging on the couch like she'd never heard a Public Warning siren in her whole life. "No. Not a single day apart."

Then she moved toward her sister with leaden steps, as if she were sinking deep underground.

Hailey fetched a mop from the tiny kitchen. She crept toward the cracked wall and its oozing black tar.

8

TAREN

Taren leaned against the outside of the house, feeling the cold seep through the back of his shirt and using it as a timer. When his back went numb, he'd go down into the bunker and get Lake out. Willow too, he guessed. However that worked.

The two of them shouldn't have gone down there. *Never go anywhere that you won't want to leave.* And now Lake was in a *bunker,* probably feeling safe and sound, hanging out with the sister she couldn't be with outside the sim.

The wall against his back was like ice.

I'll have to go down there and get her out somehow, and then the sleepers inside the house will be stuck. And all *of us will be stuck on the ship.*

Waiting.

He hated waiting.

He used his foot to push away from the side of the house. There had to be a faster way to do this.

Gravel crunched under his feet as he strode to the front door, trying to come up with an idea.

There was still the tar. What were the odds of surviving contact with it? Lake hadn't told him, didn't seem to know. Too dangerous, then.

He stopped in the middle of the driveway and shivered at the thought of the tar inside the house. Creeping over the floorboards, a spreading poison, evidence that the world had gone wrong.

He couldn't use it—but there had to be something else he could do.

He turned and looked out at the eucalyptus trees surrounding the property. Shrouded in fog, they looked almost flat. Like a backdrop.

He strode toward them, to the end of the gravel drive, just past the dark-throated shed whose door still hung open.

A curtain of fog, shadow-flat trees. Taren felt like he'd come to the edge of the world. He reached out, his skin prickling in the cold. His fingers brushed what felt like a heavy curtain.

The edge of the world. Or, at least, of this pocket of the sim.

Could he create a new pocket here? Like he had done when he'd stepped through a door into the convenience store?

Lake had said that if someone who created a pocket in the sim woke up, the pocket would close and everyone inside would wake up too. What if Taren created a new pocket and convinced everyone from the house to go inside? Then he could exit the sim—he could wake up, and wake all the other sleepers with him. A strange exit, but one that just might

work.

He pushed harder against the curtain of fog and trees and felt it stretch like a membrane. "Make a street here," he told the sim. "With that taco truck that shows up outside school on Wednesdays." *The one with the girl cashier who always smiles at me.*

The membrane stretched into a bubble that expanded, forming asphalt, the taco truck, the window where a dark-haired girl smiled at him.

Taren stared for a moment, his chest expanding as rapidly as the bubble had. *I did it.*

He looked down at his hand. *World-creator.*

It had been easy, just like dreaming up the convenience store had been.

Now all he had to do was convince the sleepers to walk into the pocket. And who wouldn't want tacos when the alternative was drinking air from an empty glass?

He jogged back to the house, breathing eucalyptus-scent and fog and triumph. "Who's hungry?" he called in the doorway. "There's a taco truck out front."

"Get like twenty and bring them in here!" Sharon called back. "There is not a single thing to eat in this house."

Taren went to stand near the couch, careful to skirt the tar still oozing over the floor. "Come get your own, it's depressing in here anyway." He couldn't even bring himself to look at whatever fresh horrors showed on the TV screen.

A boy sitting on the floor sorting through vinyl records said, "Get something for me, Sharon."

Taren wiped sweat from the back of his neck. "Everyone's going. Seriously, you should see the girl who takes the orders."

"What's a taco truck doing here while the world is literally on fire?" someone else asked.

"Maybe they don't watch the news," Sharon said, hauling herself off the couch. "Come on, last taco on Earth."

Is this really going to work? Taren watched them peel themselves from the couch and the armchairs and the massive rug that looked like it might have been loaned out by a Spanish missions museum. Sharon seemed to have forgotten all about the tar on the floor, and he had to push her away from it as she passed him, and then had to do the same for another girl who hadn't noticed it either. Then a boy in Reefs almost stepped in it and Taren froze instead of pushing him away. For a split second he thought, *It would be so much faster,* and then guilt flooded him. What if the boy didn't survive contact with the tar? Taren knocked his shoulder against him and earned a "Hey, watch it," but managed to keep the Reefs out of the tar.

Anyway, this way is just as good. Taren led them out of the house, down the gravel drive. The smell of tacos pulled them onward.

It's working.

A flash of motion at the other end of the yard caught Taren's eye. Someone was emerging from the bunker.

Not Lake.

The girl from the photo? She straightened a pack on her shoulders as she gaped at the trees. Then the house caught her attention and she beelined for it. He watched her open the front door—and vanish. Gone to another pocket of the sim. Had she meant to do that, or had she just been trying to go inside?

She'd looked like she was trying to get away from something.

Where's Lake?

He ran for the open metal door to the bunker, his nerves
firing.

A metal ladder took him down into the bunker's depths,
to another door.

"Lake?" He pushed the door open.

It wasn't what he imagined a bunker would be like. It
looked more like an underground apartment, sleeker than
any apartment he'd ever seen in person. But the opposite wall
was cracked and smeared with black paint that trailed down
to the floor, all the way to where two forms were slumped on
the couch.

"Lake?"

He lurched toward the couch, then suddenly realized—the
stuff on the floor wasn't black paint. It was tar, spread thin
over the floor but still as dark and nauseating as the thicker
stuff he'd encountered in the house. It formed a barrier between him and the couch, too wide to jump over safely.

He spied a long rug running from the living room to the
kitchen and hurried to drag it over the swath of tar. Used it as
a bridge.

"Lake, hey." She stared straight ahead, her eyes unfocused.
He knelt next to the couch and shook her shoulder. "What
happened?"

Next to her lay Willow, eyes closed but chest rising and
falling in an even rhythm.

Taren shook Lake's shoulder again and she stirred.

"It's fine," she said, frowning at him in annoyance. "We're fine here."

"You're not fine. We have to go. You can't stay here."

"Willow's here." Lake found Willow's hand and clasped it in her own. "I'm staying with her."

I'm in over my head. Taren remembered what Lake had said earlier, that she knew she was in a simulation whenever she saw Willow alive and well. He gripped the arm of the couch. Was he really going to do this? "Remember, Lake? Willow didn't make it. She's not . . ." He swallowed, hating himself. "Willow died. Remember? This isn't real."

Confusion crossed Lake's face, and then something much worse did. She seemed for a moment like something that had already shattered and would fall to pieces at the first touch.

"I'm sorry," Taren said.

"It's okay." A hard edge to her voice. The shattered pieces held together. She glanced at the figment of Willow sleeping next to her on the couch, touched the side of Willow's smooth face. She turned back to Taren, her eyes glassy. "I remember now."

Taren's chest ached.

"Come on, we should get out of here," Lake said. "Out of the sim."

Taren turned, but the rug behind him had half dissolved, the tar underneath eating away at it.

"The couch," Lake said, and at first he thought she meant they should push it across the tar, but she climbed onto the back of it and jumped over the tar-moat, easy as that. "Hurry up."

Taren jumped. Lake grabbed a potted plant from near the

door and smashed it against a granite counter so she could retrieve a shard of pottery. She scratched an X over the door.

Before she stepped through, she looked back. But not at Willow. She'd already said her goodbye to Willow for now. She looked at the damaged far wall, peered at the spiderweb of cracks as if she could read something in its pattern.

"What is it?" Taren asked.

Lake stood entranced for a moment longer. Then she shook her head. "I don't know." She stepped through the door and vanished.

Taren squinted at the cracked wall, at the floor dissolving under the swath of tar, at the empty couch where Willow had been only a moment ago.

He had a feeling Lake still had a lot to teach him about the sim, but that wasn't what was eating away like tar through his gut.

His real fear was that there was more to the sim than even Lake knew.

9

LAKE

Alone again in a stasis chamber.

Peace and quiet, Lake joked to herself. But that only made her think of Willow, sleeping on a couch in a bunker. *If only you really were safe and sound, Will.*

Lake eased out of the nest of machinery, leaned against the wall for a long moment. Her lungs made the same sound the laboring machines did. She hadn't saved one single person this time. And she'd almost lost herself to the sim.

Stupid, going into that bunker. She'd seen the girl's face in the photo and had thought, *If Willow were trapped, I'd want someone to save her.*

She pressed her sweaty forehead against the cool wall. *Is that why you brought Willow down with you? You wanted to feel like you were saving her?*

Only the rich and lucky survived.

Lake had never been rich. And one day, she knew, her luck would run out, just like Taren had said.

She slid the door open.

A hand shot out and pulled her into the warehouse. "It's just me," Taren said into her ear. Salt-and-metal smell, familiar to anyone who spent time sleeping inside machines.

"What're you doing?" Lake stumbled after him, surprised at his grip on her wrist.

He stopped near the door of the warehouse and peered out, looking for trouble. "I did it. I woke the sleepers from the house. They'll be coming out of their stasis chambers. We don't want them to see us, right? They'll tell."

"You did what?" She marveled at the lights in the warehouse. They were brighter, no longer flickering like the lights in the hallway.

"I made a pocket in the sim, like you showed me. Right at the edge of the pocket we were in. I convinced them all to go inside the pocket I made, and now—I'm awake, the pocket's closed. Which means they're waking up now too. Right?"

Lake stared at him. At the flickering light from the hallway pulsing in his anxious eyes. "You got all the partiers from the house to go inside a pocket you made?" she said, keeping her voice low.

Taren nodded. He eased into the hallway, and Lake followed, alert for the sound of distant footsteps. "But we didn't wake the girl in the bunker," Taren admitted.

"No, we didn't. I messed that up." Lake couldn't look at him while she said it. "She mentioned a place called the Battery. I think that's where most of the sleepers have headed."

"What battery? There are dozens in San Francisco."

"I don't know." Lake stopped short of the corner. "Most of

them are just concrete-lined holes in the ground, or rusted gun mounts. Can't be very many that are big enough for a group of people to camp in."

"Why would they want to? I don't think any of the batteries around the city have been in use for at least a century. It's not like they're stocked with supplies."

"But a battery *feels* safe," Lake said. "That's all that matters to sleepers." She pictured the flowerpot smashed on the counter, dirt scattered over the floor. "By the way, thanks for coming in after me when I got stuck in that bunker."

They'd pressed themselves against the wall of the hallway, and Taren's arm shook next to hers. Nerves, adrenaline, thirst. "Your sister . . ."

"I don't want to talk about it." Lake peeled herself away from the wall. "We should split up, take different hallways. Less suspicious that way."

Taren opened his mouth to say something but apparently thought better of it. He slinked around the corner, leaving Lake to listen for the distant click of opening stasis chambers and the stumbling footsteps of newly wakened sleepers.

Instead, she heard Taren shouting from around the corner. "Hey, get off me!"

Shit. The assholes from the eatery must have been waiting.

Lake had no way to help Taren. No way to get out of this hallway without them spotting her as well.

And—

Shit again. She could hear them coming for her now.

She turned and hurtled toward the warehouse.

Ran to the closest stasis chamber. It was locked.

She tried another, and another. Finally—one that was un-locked. She slid the panel shut behind her and locked herself in. Eased herself into the bed. The nodes engaged at her temples. Darkness.

PARACOSM.

Back home, she'd been good at the app's VR game. Peaceful mode, just for building simulated houses and exploring weird landscapes other users had created. Good practice for what she was meant to do now: figure out how to live on a planet still scabbed over by war.

"Except that's not what you're good for at all, is it?" She said it out loud, even though it was weird to talk to a computer program.

It was her nerves. *I almost got trapped, Taren had to save me.*

She'd just stay long enough for the mob from the eatery to get bored waiting for her.

Then, right back out to return the favor and spring Taren.

The penny pub's copper walls winked like fireflies. The coin still spun on the bar. A penny from the wall? It seemed too large for that. She used an empty glass to pin it flat. The thick glass magnified an image on the coppery metal: a tree in relief. An *odd* tree, with a billowing crown.

The image sparked something in her brain. Just as that girl's story had. *"Trees with blue and purple leaves that the sun shines right through."*

The place Lake saw so often in her dreams.

She picked up the coin and rubbed her finger over the

metal tree, her thoughts racing. She'd seen plenty of evidence that the sim responded to thoughts and feelings. But was it mining even her dreams now? Hers and the girl's from the bunker?

And why was it here in Ransom's pub?

She crossed to the door. As the hinges creaked, she closed her eyes to wish for a certain sight to greet her.

She stepped through the door onto soft sand.

In the distance, Ransom stood under the pier, a shadow under shadows. He was skipping rocks over the surf, a fact Lake barely registered as she shed her boots and ran toward him, dodging charred bits of firewood and then clumps of seaweed. He started when she tackled him from behind and wrapped her arms around him.

"I went to the penny pub to check on you," she said. Her heart beat right against his back.

"I didn't want to hang around there." He turned so he could pull her against his chest. "Didn't want to find out who was banging on the door."

"It was only someone in the stasis warehouse, coming to check if I was all right. Not someone in the sim after all." Lake twined her fingers in his shirt. "Have you been here just waiting for me?"

"I figured you'd know where to find me." He nodded at the crumbling cliffs in the distance like castle ruins jutting onto the beach. "That's the first place I ever saw you. You were up there searching for something in those rocks."

The staggered platforms of mudstone gleamed in the sun, wet with sea spray. This was one of the first places Lake had wandered into after she'd come out of stasis and into the sim. She remembered climbing over the rough rock, crouching, peering past fronded anemones and flat strands of kelp. Searching . . .

"I saw you up on the rocks, and I was worried for you," Ransom said. "I knew you had lost something."

Lake touched the thread bracelet circling her wrist.

"I waited for you to come down," he said.

"You waited and waited, and the sun never moved in the sky. That's how I knew this place wasn't real." *But it looks just like the coast back home, where Willow once begged to search the tide pools, and Mom made me promise not to lose her . . .*

The salty air stung Lake's throat.

"What made you come here that day?" Lake asked. "Why this beach?" *Could we have met here once in real life, as kids, and we've never known it?*

Ransom let go of her to pick up another rock from the sand and chuck it toward the water. "I hate it when you do that."

"Try to get to know you?"

"So you can give me a gift you think will save me from the sim. But it never works."

"You don't think I want to know about how you grew up just so I can know? Whether you played basketball or liked to swim or ate your weight in ice cream every summer?"

"You can know a person by being with them here and now."

Can you? Lake took the coin from her pocket. "Where did this come from?"

Ransom accepted it from her and examined the strange tree stamped on its face.

"A sleeper told me about a place in the sim with trees like the one on this coin. Like the ones in my dreams." Lake was shaking, and not from the chill of the wind. "Except—I don't think they were dreams. I think I must have gone there."

Ransom studied the coin a moment longer. Then he slipped it into his pocket. "Just the sim, manifesting my guilt." His eyes were hard and flat as the seawater in the distance.

"So you *have* heard about this place. It exists? Here in the sim?" She stepped back from him. "Why didn't you tell me?"

"Because . . ." He rubbed a hand over his forehead and left a trail of sand over his skin. "I was afraid you'd go looking for it. Another endless quest to keep you out of the real world."

Lake watched the wet sand at her feet, where tiny holes opened as the water slid away. A miniature crab churned beneath the surface. "I come to the sim to wake the sleepers. I do it because I'm good at it, and because no one else will."

"And because you want to be with Willow."

Lake's stomach twisted. "Can you blame me?"

Ransom stepped close again. He pressed his forehead against hers, and she felt the dusting of sand there. "Not one bit."

She tipped her head back so she could look up at him. Only the warmth of his arms closing around her kept away the chill her next words gave her: "I found out where the sleepers are all going. I have to follow them there, to get them free."

Ransom's arms went stiff around her. Dread flooded his gaze.

"They'll never come out on their own," Lake said. "There must be dozens of them hunkering down together, keeping each other trapped."

Ransom stared into the distance, like he hadn't heard her. But the next moment, he hugged her tighter and said, "Let me go to the Battery for you. It's not like I'm getting out of the sim anytime soon anyway."

Lake's breath went hard in her lungs. She didn't *want* to go to the Battery. She didn't want to risk losing herself to the sim, which she knew was all too possible in such a large pocket. If she let Ransom go instead, if he could wake the sleepers himself . . .

She shook her head. "You've never woken a sleeper before."

"It's hard to, when you hardly meet them."

"And how would you get to the Battery? You get stuck, you can't always get where you want to go in the sim."

He let go of her, frowning.

"You take the gifts I give you," Lake went on, because the heat in her chest wouldn't let her stop, "and you follow me through doors and you still don't wake up on the ship."

"Doesn't that prove there's too much about the sim you don't understand? That the best thing to do is leave it behind for good?"

"I *have* to go to the Battery. No one else can do it."

"You *want* to go. You want a reason to spend more time with Willow." Ransom shook his head. "I've tried so many times to tell you . . ."

That Willow isn't good for me. Lake wrapped her arms around herself, cold and miserable.

"But as long as she's part of the sim, you won't want to leave her." Ransom leaned to pluck something from the sand. When he straightened, he held out his palm to show her a sun-bleached sand dollar. Perfectly whole, a rare find in the real world. Though maybe not so rare in a simulation. "They say it's good luck. Maybe it'll help you with the Battery."

She didn't take it from him. "That day the sun never set, you brought me things washed up on the sand. Because you knew I was looking for something, missing something." *Someone.* "The sun never set, and you kept bringing me things, and it was the only day of my life I knew what forever would feel like. And you were there, so forever didn't feel bad."

"I know why you were searching that day. You keep trying to find everyone who's stuck in the sim, but there's only one person you're really looking for."

Lake pushed his hand with the sand dollar back toward him.

"If you keep following Willow deeper into the sim," he said, "you'll never come out."

Freezing black seawater crept over Lake's toes. A cold feeling crept into her chest. "And what about you? Will you ever find your way out of the sim?"

Ransom put his arms around her again, and he was a shield from the cold wind, if not from the cold thoughts edging into her mind. "Why would I want to leave?" he said. "If this is where you are?"

She let him go on holding her, but she knew that wasn't an answer. Ransom never had answers. And one day, she'd have to find out why.

10

TAREN

The smell inside the ship's locked dining room reminded Taren of the ocean. Not in a good way.

He'd been sitting on the floor, because someone had removed all the chairs and the table. Sleeping with his head tipped back against the wall, dreaming of pizza and hammocks and other things that he had only ever found on the planet turning below him. The yellow light of living room lamps. His mom's off-key singing, his dad's elbow nudges.

He'd wakened to the smell of fishy water and the shock of it seeping into his pants.

He scrambled to his feet. A half-inch of water stood on the floor. Leaking from where? That smell—like the algae drinks he'd forced down.

"Hey!" He banged a fist against the glass door and glared at the group of boys dissecting a cleaning bot on a nearby table. One of them gave him a bored look and went back to his work.

Taren used the side of his foot to send the water under the

door. Waited a minute. The closest boy looked up in surprise when the water reached his bare feet. He came and peered into the locked room.

"You've got a broken pump in your algae tank," Taren shouted to him.

The boy frowned. He turned back to say something to his friends.

Taren banged on the glass again. "Hey. I can fix it."

"You?" The boy looked him over.

Skinny, weak, and wet, I know.

But his brother had taught him about fixing things.

"You want to lose your food supply?" Taren shouted through the glass. He kicked more water under the door to underscore the situation's urgency.

The boys abandoned their project to drag the barricade away from Taren's door. "You know what you're doing?" one of them asked.

"I know how to unclog a pump and change a filter. I have a fish tank at home, for one thing." *Had, whatever.*

They led him through a doorway to a mad-scientist lab. Endless yards of white lights and tubing. Column after column of bright green bulbs stacked to the ceiling—the algae tanks. Horrible sucking and groaning that confirmed Taren's fears that something had broken.

He lifted a section of tubing clogged with green clumps. "Pretty sure this is supposed to pump in the other direction," he told the boys who still huddled close like prison guards. "See if you can find the generator. Sounds like it's dying."

"You can fix it, though?" one of the boys asked.

Fix a space-generator? Was he supposed to have had practice at that?

He turned to glance at the boy, whose face was smudged with grease from the dissected cleaner bot. Hands were black with it. Taren couldn't help but think of his brother, genius mechanic. *"Can you fix it or can't you?"* his brother used to say when he schooled Taren in car repairs, a teasing smirk on his grease-streaked face.

"What's your name?" Taren asked the boy.

"Shawn."

"Just find the generator, Shawn," Taren said. "We'll start there."

"Is this it?" One of the other boys was squinting at a metal grid sliding up and down.

"That looks like some kind of press, probably for extracting water from the algae," Taren said.

The boy gave him an uncertain look.

"Or could be a torture device," Taren said. *How would I know?*

"Well, there's no algae on it."

"Second guess was right then," Taren muttered. At the boy's anxious glance, he said, "I think it's broken. Like the pump."

"It smells like death."

"Like *our* death, specifically," another boy said.

Taren heard Gray's voice in his head: *"Can you fix it or can't you?"*

He leaned over the tank with the metal grid. A smell like rotten eggs made him gag. "I think the algae's getting trapped somewhere and going bad."

"So what do we do?"

Taren looked out over the glass forest of algae tanks, the yards of tubing, the foreign machinery. *We get the hell off this ship.* "What about the protein bars?" he asked. "Where are those stored?"

The boys exchanged dark looks with one another. "We divided them up," Shawn said.

"Okay? And put them where?"

More dark looks. "We're not telling you."

The pumps groaned, echoing Taren's empty stomach. "All this algae is going to rot in the tanks. The protein bars are all we have."

Shawn forced it out: "There isn't enough left for everyone."

"For everyone to what?" Taren's water-soaked clothes made him shiver. "For everyone to eat for a month? A couple weeks?"

"There aren't enough for everyone to eat. A bunch of us have three or four stashed away for sharing with our friends. Then—that's it."

"That's . . . it?" Taren was sinking right through the watery floor, into someplace dark and cold. The rotting-fish smell flooded his lungs.

"Can you fix it or can't you?"

Too bad it's not you on this ship, Gray.

"You said you could fix it," Shawn reminded him.

A broken pump, maybe. A complete lack of food and a whole busted lab?

Taren gripped the edge of the stinking tank, tried to fight the urgent fear boiling through him. The pillars of slowly rotting algae were the diseased bones of the ship, the smell of it the signal of his own coming death.

We have to get off this ship.

I have to get them all out of the sim, and we have to get out of here as fast as possible.

"I can fix it," he said. *Not the tanks—but I can get people out of the sim.* "Just . . . clear out and let me try some things."

They exchanged looks again. Probably sensed he was lying and just wanted to get free from them.

"I can't do shit if I'm locked in the eatery," he told them.

They didn't argue. Taren listened to the water slosh under their feet as they trudged out of the lab. He stared at the columns of rotting food and felt something inside him rot along with it.

I can fix it. Not the ship, but I can get people out. Haven't I proved that?

He had to find Lake.

They had to get to the Battery.

11

TAREN

Taren stayed in the lab long enough to make sure the other boys wouldn't notice him leaving. Then he went to the stasis warehouse to find Lake.

The maze of chambers. The hum of machinery like the wheeze of a beast. Taren had walked through worse dreams, but this was the only nightmare he had come back to voluntarily.

"Lake?" he whispered at a huddled form slumped against a chamber.

Lake lifted her head, looked like hell in the low light. Would probably look worse in brighter. "You got away. What's that smell?"

"Our food supply going to shit. I checked on the algae tanks. It's all rotting." He almost didn't tell her more, she already looked so completely stricken. "Only a handful of protein bars left. No sign of any other food on board, unless you know of something?"

She shook her head, her eyes in shadow. "We have to go to the Battery."

He couldn't argue. But her weary slump had him worried. "You don't look like you're ready to go back in."

She pushed herself to her feet. "I'm fine."

"Gotten any sleep recently?" He handed her one of the cups of water he'd brought with him.

"A little, but . . ."

"You had that dream again? Something chasing you?"

She started to drink, paused. "I'm not going to lie. I think plugging into a broken sim might not be the greatest thing for a girl's brain." She took her time draining the cup while Taren used the silence to stew in anxiety.

"Everyone has weird dreams," he said finally, trying to reassure mostly himself. He handed her a protein bar he'd slipped out of one of the boys' pockets in the lab. "You seem like you need this more than I do."

"I got my fill in the sim," she joked, and tried to hand it back.

"Me too," he lied. "Fifty tacos. And what do you know, this protein bar is taco-flavored."

She smiled in a way that said she didn't believe him but she'd eat it anyway. He set the second cup of water next to the stasis chamber, in case they needed it when they woke later.

"Hey, do you remember where you went in the sim before you set up camp in the zoo?" Lake asked.

"My house."

"And before that?"

He shrugged. "Maybe that's where I started." But he'd been someplace before that—he could remember wanting to go find his house. "I don't know. It's like when you have different dreams, one after another. But when you wake up, you only really remember the last one."

She didn't say anything, just chewed thoughtfully.

"Why do you ask?"

"I've got most of the sim mentally mapped," she said. "But I think there might be pockets I've been to that I don't remember."

Taren wiped his sweaty palms on his pants. "Pockets with sleepers? How many sleepers did you say are left in the sim?"

"Fifty-two, judging by the names on the eatery wall that I haven't marked off yet. Minus the sleepers you rescued from that house." She stopped chewing, looked troubled.

"What?" Taren prompted.

"Nothing. Just . . . there's a name I keep looking for and never finding." Taren was about to ask which name, but she barreled on. "Maybe that means there are sleepers in the sim that no one knows about? People who came on board without any friends or siblings?"

He had a feeling she had someone specific in mind, but something else had captured his attention. He moved to examine the next chamber over, lifted a hand to trace a dent in the battered panel that sealed the chamber shut.

"Don't let anyone tell you we haven't tried to get at the sleepers inside," Lake said in explanation.

"Why do the panels even lock?"

"Probably only supposed to open for medical personnel. Which we lack."

"That's a shit-stupid oversight."

"Theories are: A, medical personnel were here, awake the

whole time and taking care of us, but we've been asleep so long they died. And B, medical personnel are still here but they're stuck in the sim."

"Which do you subscribe to?"

"I've seen no dead bodies on the ship and no adults in the sim."

"Then I stand by what I said."

"I should mention there are areas of the sim I have yet to visit."

"Like the Battery."

A long pause while Lake carefully brushed crumbs from her palms. "And a couple other places."

"Such as?"

She shook her head. "We've wasted enough time." She set the empty cup inside the open door of her stasis chamber.

Taren glanced in at the chamber, suddenly itching to get going. But there was something Lake wasn't telling him, judging by her stiff movements. "I don't think I can afford any more surprises from you in the sim."

She froze. Taren almost regretted what he'd said. But then she leaned against the doorway and said, "There's one pocket in the sim we can't ever go to. If you ever see me try to go there, or if . . . if Willow tries to get me to go . . ."

"Why would Willow—?"

"Just—don't ever let me go through the door in the middle of the Mojave Desert, okay?"

Across the warehouse, some machinery stalled and restarted with a grumble like a wakening beast.

"What's in—"

"Enough doom talk for now, okay?" Lake cut in. "Let's just go."

I don't think I want to know, anyway. "We don't know which battery we're going to," he reminded her.

"I have an idea of which one we should try."

"So do I. Muir Beach Overlook. It's pretty secluded. If that's where the sleepers are camped, it makes sense that you wouldn't have stumbled across it."

"Never been there in real life," Lake said. "Might be hard for me to go there first thing. Let's start in that sim neighborhood near Sixteenth Avenue again and decide where to go from there. Just picture it while you're going under and you should end up there."

"Wait, what if I *don't* end up there?"

"You made it there last time just fine."

Taren nodded, but in his mind, he saw his brother's teasing smirk.

I can do this, Gray.

If Lake and I can both keep our grip on reality.

So he was talking to his brother now, like Lake did with Willow. That didn't seem like the best sign.

Lake turned, heading into her stasis chamber.

"Wait," Taren said, and Lake reappeared in the doorway. "If we wake the sleepers in the Battery, will you be able to leave the sim? If it means saying goodbye to your sister?"

Lake's eyes blazed. She turned and disappeared into her chamber, leaving Taren with the phantom of the pain he'd caused her. *Haven't you already hurt her enough?* he scolded himself. *Do you have to keep reminding her that her sister is dead?*

And yet, he might have to, if he hoped to leave the Battery, leave the sim.

He moved to his own chamber, his legs heavy and numb. He lowered himself onto the electronic altar of the stasis bed, and tried not to think about whether Lake would be able to make herself leave Willow behind. He knew what it was like to see the people you most loved only when you dreamed . . .

Moments later, or maybe days—he couldn't keep it straight—he found himself standing at the end of a lonely staircase on a bluff overlooking the ocean. He knew it was the Pacific because he knew exactly where he was: Muir Beach Overlook, across the Golden Gate Bridge from San Francisco. He used to come here with his family—Mom and Dad and Gray. They'd drive over the bridge, up Highway 1, stop at places like this to take in the shape of the world, measure its edges.

He gazed down at the water, mesmerized by the seafoam blooming around the rocks. *How did I get here?* He had a feeling he was supposed to be somewhere else, that he was supposed to meet someone.

He turned against the wooden railing, searching. Someone was coming down the winding steps to meet him, a dark figure against the sun. Not Mom or Dad, coming to listen to the waves crash with him—

"Gray?" Taren called.

His brother grinned back at him, the sun a bright disk behind his head. "Always racing to the end of the stairs. You're supposed to stop and take in the views along the way."

Taren meant to answer, but his voice caught in his throat.

The wind ruffled Gray's hair, the sleeves of his T-shirt, the feathery scrub at his feet as if to say, *Everything is alive.*

"One day we'll convince Mom and Dad we should bike out here," Gray said. He reached the bottom of the stairs and slung an arm around Taren's neck, messed up Taren's already wind-mussed hair.

"Dad would never make it," Taren said into Gray's shirt while trying not to breathe in the smell of Gray's sweat. He'd usually squirm away from Gray, duck out of his brother's reach. But he didn't want to this time. He felt like it'd been a million years since they'd last been together. A million and one.

"You've been out here for ages," Gray said, releasing him.

"I have?"

Gray's mood shifted. He shoved his hands into his pockets and grimaced against the cold. "Why have you been wasting so much time?"

Taren clutched the wooden railing. He looked out at the foamy coastline stretching toward the city so far away. "I didn't mean to. I want to go home." His voice sounded high and babyish to his own ears. How must it sound to Gray?

"You've been gone a long time," Gray said. "You went on that ship, and you never came back."

Taren raked his fingers over his head. He was starting to remember. He'd gotten a spot on a ship by sheer luck. And now it was time to go home—but the ship wouldn't let him. It was locking itself up, shutting down, closing around him like a fist that would squeeze the life out of him.

"You slept for decades," Gray went on. "That's all you do—sleep. You don't care about leaving the ship."

"The ship won't *let* me leave," Taren said. "Not until every last person is awake."

"Then you'd better wake them. *Fast.*"

"I'm trying to. They're stuck—trapped in a simulation." The sight of the rippling hillside suddenly made him dizzy. The fluttering fennel, the swaying cypresses. *I'm in a simulation?* "I'm going to fix things."

"You think *you* can fix anything?" Gray gave a derisive snort. "If I were on that ship, I'd clear out the sim so fast. I'd do whatever it took."

"I wish you could help me."

"You don't have time for wishing. The ship is breaking down. You're going to die."

Taren squeezed his eyes shut. "No, I can do this. I just have to—"

"You've been out here for ages. Why have you been wasting so much time?"

Taren opened his eyes. "You said that already." He watched Gray shove his hands in his pockets again. Watched the wind ruffle his sleeves the same way it had a minute ago. "You're saying the same things over and over."

"You went on that ship," Gray said. "You slept for decades—"

"Stop."

It wasn't his brother.

Gray was a figment.

"You think *you* can fix anything?" he said.

"You're not real," Taren said. "You're part of the sim." How did the sim know those things about his family?

It had read his mind. It had found his worst fears, his deepest guilt: An empty house. An angry brother. An impossible task.

Things no one had a right to know. Or to shove back in his face.

Taren's anger rose, whipped up like seafoam by wind.

"You're nothing," Taren said to the ghost before him. "You think I can't clear the sim? You don't know what I can do." He wanted to stick his fist out and see if it would go right through the figment of his brother. Something stopped him. The lines on Gray's squinting face, the goose bumps on his wind-chilled arms.

The figment of Gray frowned, uncertain in the face of Taren's anger. "If I were on that ship . . ."

"Go away," Taren said through gritted teeth.

From the steps along the bluff's ridge, someone called Taren's name. He shaded his eyes with his hand.

Lake.

Taren turned to the figment. "Go away," he barked.

The figment slinked toward the railing. It cowered there a moment, looking between Taren and the distant figure coming down the steps. "You don't have much time," the figment told Taren. Then it climbed over the railing and disappeared.

Taren drew in a steadying breath.

"Hey," Lake said, stopping just before the end of the staircase. "I thought I lost you. Who was that?"

Taren inched toward the railing. He searched in vain for the figment on the steep incline below. "No one. A figment."

At the top of the ridge, Willow called, "Picnic over yet?"

"We were supposed to meet in the sim neighborhood," Lake told Taren.

"I got mixed up." The rippling scrub that covered the incline kept catching his eye and making his heart pound. *That wasn't Gray. That wasn't my brother.*

My brother wouldn't say those things.

But that didn't matter, did it? Because even if that had only been a figment of his brother, the things it had said were still true. Taren would die soon if he didn't clear the sim.

"When I didn't see you in the neighborhood, I figured you jumped the gun and came here," Lake said.

Taren barely heard her. He was still scanning the scrub-and-rock incline so steep it would surely send any climbers to their death.

"Hey, you okay?" Lake asked.

Taren forced himself to look away from the railing. "I don't like it here. Let's go."

Lake studied his face a moment longer. Taren almost couldn't stand the concern in her eyes. "Were you worried I'd lost you?" she asked.

"Don't feel sorry for me, I don't deserve it. I should have tried harder."

"Hey." Lake touched his arm and he tried not to shrink away. "Don't be so hard on yourself. You're doing okay."

Taren brushed past her and started climbing the stairs. "We need better than *okay* if we're going to clear the sim."

12

LAKE

They found the nearest door—a public bathroom near the top of the stairs—and Taren stepped through alone to find a place to change his appearance. When he came back, sporting scruffy facial hair that Lake tried not to laugh at, he asked, "Why's it always San Francisco? Couldn't the sim be *anything*?"

"You don't like San Francisco?" Willow asked.

"I like it fine. I just don't get why I never end up on a nice tropical island, or at a hockey game."

"Poor guy," Willow said. "All you ever get is the two of us."

He couldn't help smiling. "A computer program and a walking alarm clock. Honestly, I've had weirder friends."

"Thanks?" Lake said. "Anyway, everyone on the ship came from San Francisco, and that's where we all want to get back to. So that's what the sim gives us."

"To get us ready to go home," Taren said.

"Sure." *That's what the sim is supposed to do, anyway. Doesn't seem like that's what's happening.* Lake gestured for them to step aside so she could ready herself to step through the door. "I didn't see any sleepers at your overlook. So we'll try my idea next, okay?"

Lake tried to envision the Battery, preparing to step through the door. Or anyway, she tried to picture the set of concrete pits she guessed was the place where everyone was gathering.

Taren was still lingering at the corner of her vision, twitching with nervous energy. "There's a landing strip at SFO for spaceships?" he asked, his voice pitched oddly high.

He was opening too many cans for his own good.

"Actually," Lake said, "we took a poll on the ship, and everyone figures the shuttles will probably land in the bay."

"Shit," Taren said. "You don't know. Nobody knows?"

"You like standing in front of public bathrooms all day?" Lake asked.

But Willow seemed to feel bad for him. She took his hand in hers and said, "There are so many things in general you don't know, Taren. So many." She smiled like it should make him feel better.

At least it stopped him talking.

Lake pulled the door open, picturing concrete pits and empty gun mounts—the Battery. And its neighboring red-roof buildings, shaded by eucalyptus—the Presidio, a decent place to start a survivors' town. *That has to be the place everyone's gone.* She reached back and grabbed Taren's free hand and pulled him through.

"This can't be the place," Taren said, his hand going rigid in hers.

"When I think *battery,* I think *presidio.* You?"

"This is the Presidio?"

Lake tried not to picture the place as it had once been—big blocky buildings with cheerful red tile roofs, framed with palm trees and shaded by groves of eucalyptus. The trees were gone now. The buildings, blackened shells. The whole place had been ravaged by the same firestorms she and Taren had seen on TV at the sim-house party.

"No way there's anyone sheltering here," Taren said.

"But this has to be it, right?" Willow asked. "How many more batteries can San Francisco have?"

"A *lot,*" Taren said.

Willow scowled at him, annoyed. "Okay, thanks, *professor.* Lake's doing her best."

Lake drew in a slow breath, trying to think. She had imagined sleepers flocking here to camp in abandoned buildings and hide out in the batteries along the coastal edge of the old fort. "It just made sense that this would be the right place," she said. "The other batteries around the coastline are only concrete shells. Not worth living in, especially if you've got several dozen people with you."

"What do we do now?" Taren took in the blackened landscape with the misery of a cleanup crew. "Check every battery, one by one?"

"I bet it'll go faster if we split up," Willow said, still annoyed with him.

Lake couldn't think what to do. She could only stare at the black husks of buildings, and the empty horizon where eucalyptus branches had once split sunshine into long streamers.

Is this what's waiting for us back home?

I should have guessed a beautiful place like this would be gone.

"Do you smell that?" Taren asked.

Smoke. Lake looked up at the gray cloud sliding over the sun, turning it to a molten blot. "The firestorm. It's coming back."

"That doesn't make any sense," Taren said. "This place has already burned down."

Lake held her palm up, as if to catch rain. Flakes of white ash drifted down to settle on her skin like the ghost of snow. "It's going to burn again, somehow. We better go."

She turned back the way they had come, eaten up by frustration. *This whole trip has been a failure, and now we have to leave.*

She froze. She should have thought about this—

They'd come here through a door, of course. And here was that door, waiting for them. In a *building*. A square white building, miraculously unmarked by smoke, though its roof was nothing but naked beams.

Taren inspected a plank nailed to the wall. *Supplies on Credit,* it proclaimed in carved letters. "It's some kind of trading post, I think."

"A postapocalyptic store?" Willow darted to touch the sign, as if considering it for a souvenir. "I bet they sell zombie-hunting stuff."

"Sleepers are zombies enough," Lake said. "And we don't *hunt* them."

She walked up to the rough-hewn door. No knob, just a

block of wood to grip when you needed to pull the door shut. "I think there are people inside," she said. Voices drifted up through the skeleton roof.

"Is this the Battery after all?" Taren asked, though he sounded like he didn't believe it.

Willow peered at him. "Do you know what a battery is? Gun mounts and concrete and all that?"

"It doesn't look big enough to hold fifty sleepers," Lake said, "but there might be someone inside who can tell us where the Battery is."

"What about the fire?" Taren said, lifting his gaze to the drifting smoke.

"Just make sure to tell me when the sky turns red." Lake ignored Taren's incredulous look and cracked open the door. Figures sat hunched at a table. She pushed the door open farther and stepped inside, her boots muffled by the ash that carpeted the floor.

"I never know when to expect a door to take us into a room," Taren said, edging in behind her, "instead of into another places."

"It depends on who's opening the door," Lake said, "and what they envision."

She looked around. It was really two tables, and four times as many strangers, some of them playing cards at the tables, one leaning over a sale counter, one scanning the shelves that lined every wall. Flakes of ash drifted down between bare roof beams, unnoticed.

No one looked up when Lake and her crew walked in.

The teen girl behind the counter called teasingly to one of

the cardplayers, "You have a pair. Everyone knows you have a pair when you grimace like that."

The boy glared at her and slapped his cards onto the table. The other cardplayers laughed. Their clothes were ripped, their necks black with dirt, faces speckled with ash. They still hadn't looked up at the newcomers.

"Mind if we come in?" Lake asked.

The girl behind the counter gave her a perfunctory smile. "We do credit if your name's good. Otherwise, we do trades. We don't take promises."

"I've sworn off those anyway," Lake said. She eyed the teens at both tables while she pretended to be interested in the odd offerings teetering on the shelves: wind-up flashlights and pliers and huge cans of food and boxes of infant formula. Something was off here. The girl in the splintered chair was staring at the table instead of at the cards she held. The boy across the room studied a shelf without picking anything up.

"We're shopping?" Taren whispered as Lake picked over the shelves. "Do you remember there's a firestorm heading this way?"

"I'm getting a feel for the crowd," Lake murmured.

Willow leaned in to say, "Is it just me or is everyone here giving off a weird vibe?"

Taren and Lake turned in time to see a boy at one of the tables lift a tin cup to his lips, ignore the flakes of ash that fell into his drink, and take a swig.

Something's definitely wrong here.

The door opened and a boy in a ratty trucker cap leaned

in. "Where do you want me to stack the firewood I collected?" Didn't seem to notice three strangers standing nearby. But maybe strangers were common around here.

"Side of the building," the girl behind the counter said, "where people can see we have it."

He disappeared, and Lake couldn't hold off any longer. "Any idea where we can find the Battery?" she asked the shopkeeper behind the counter.

But the girl didn't seem to hear her. Her attention went to a boy who'd been browsing the shelves since Lake had walked in.

"What are you looking for, Ryan?" the girl called.

"Got any more boxes of those waterproof matches?"

Taren lifted his eyebrows and muttered to Lake, "He could just wait five minutes—these roof beams are about to turn into matchsticks."

Lake coughed against the ash in her throat. "We need to figure out whose bad mood is manifesting disaster. See if we can head it off."

"What do you mean?" Taren asked.

"We need to figure out who here is the dreamer, the one who created this place. That person is turning this place into a firepit, whether they mean to or not."

"Who do you think it is?" Taren asked. "Shopkeeper, maybe?"

"Could be anyone," Willow said.

We don't have time for this. We need to find out about the Battery and leave. "Hey," Lake called out to the room, "anyone here know how to get to the Battery?"

The girl at the counter gave her a blank look, but a boy at a table perked up. Lake turned to him. "You know the place I'm talking about?"

He held his cards higher, a fence to hide behind, and shook his head.

What's going on?

"Maybe we should just get out of here," Willow said. "I don't like this place." White-gray flakes had gathered in her hair, on her sleeves.

Lake looked down and saw speckles on her own clothes. Smoke clouded her lungs.

The door squealed open again. "Where do you want me to stack the firewood I collected?"

"Side of the building, where people can see we have it."

Lake's gaze snapped to Taren's.

"You have a pair," the girl behind the counter said.

"Everyone knows you have a pair when you grimace like that," Lake finished for her.

Slap of cards hitting the table.

Laughter.

"Everyone here's a figment," Lake said, her veins turning to ice. *How is this possible?*

"Do figments just hang out and go through scenes together even when no one's here to see it?" Taren asked.

"*We're* here," Willow said.

"They were talking before we walked in," Lake said, fighting the squirming in her stomach. "I heard them."

"That doesn't make any sense," Taren said. "Programs don't just run for their own amusement. Do they?"

Lake looked up again at the fluttering ashfall. "This place is stuck in a loop."

"Why? What's causing it?" Taren's voice was heavy with dread.

The girl at the counter said, "Ryan, in the *back*."

"*You* go back there," Ryan replied sourly. "Isn't that supposed to be *your* job?"

Lake thought her nerves might split when the door squealed again and Ratty Cap called, "Where do you want me to stack the firewood I collected?"

"Side of the building," Lake murmured.

What's causing it? Good question.

She pushed past Ratty Cap and went outside, around to the prime spot for firewood—

A black clump, like a cluster of mold spores, clung to the white side of the building. Lake crouched to see it better. *Not mold.* It squirmed and crawled over itself, shifting its shape over and over, like something trying and failing to hold form.

Lake fell back onto the asphalt, grit pricking her bare legs, same as the horror pricking her chest.

And what's in the back of the store, where Ryan doesn't want to go?

The boy with the ratty cap came out and walked past her, over to a jumble of thin branches. He froze, staring at the tar, his head twitching from side to side like he couldn't comprehend what he was seeing. Lake slowly got to her feet and backed away.

The door squealed open again. "Lake," Taren said from the doorway, "I—I found something."

She knew from the dread in his voice. She knew what he'd found. Her knees threatened to buckle.

She slid past him and walked back into the trading post. Ducked under the counter, found the doorway to the stockroom—

And almost emptied her stomach.

Here, the squirming black residue wasn't a clump of mold or a shifting spot.

It was a mass the size of a cat, pulsing and flexing inside an open lead box. As it shifted, the box did, the sides bulging out of shape and then flattening again.

"How did it all get here?" Taren asked, his voice choked with the same disgust Lake felt.

"Someone's stockpiling it. That's the reason for the bad feeling in this place." She turned back to the doorway. "Where's Willow?"

But then she froze.

Behind Taren, in the stockroom's doorway, stood the boy who'd hid behind his hand of cards.

It's true, Lake thought. *The program doesn't run for itself.*

The boy's gaze shifted from Taren to Lake. "You were asking about the Battery?"

Taren turned to face him, took a wary step back, into the room. "You know where it is?"

The boy tugged at a sweat-darkened bandana around his neck. "They won't let you in without someone to vouch for you."

"You . . ." Taren looked uncertain. "You could vouch for us."

Lake sensed the tar squirming behind her in its box.

"Haven't seen you around here before," the boy said. He leaned a little to one side, flicked his gaze in the direction of the tar.

It's him, he's the one who's stockpiling it. Why?

Ash drifted in the air between them, tinged with red. Lake looked up at the glowing sky. *Fire's coming.*

No time for games.

She turned sideways so he could have a proper view of the tar. "Do you know what this is?" she asked him.

"Does anyone," he said flatly.

"Do you know what it'll *do*?"

"Snuff you out of existence. Much faster than any firestorm will."

"Then why are you stockpiling it?" Taren asked the boy.

"For protection." The boy inched into the room and Lake saw now that he held one of the sturdy sticks from outside, a broken bit of branch. A weapon.

Lake's stomach twisted. "Protection from what?"

The makeshift club twitched in the boy's hand. "There was a girl here with you—your sister?" His expression was as stony as if he were still trying to out-poker a computer program.

Where is *Willow?*

"You have to get rid of this stuff," Lake said, jabbing her hand in the direction of the tar.

The broken branch twitched again. "There's a girl who comes around. Sometimes has a younger sister with her. And wherever she goes, death follows."

Lake's throat tightened.

"People vanish," the boy went on. "Just like when a person touches *that*." He pointed his club at the box behind Lake.

Lake looked to Taren. She could tell by his widening eyes that he was starting to grasp what the boy was saying.

They think I'm their enemy.

"One day," the boy went on, "she'll come for the Battery. She'll come for every last one of us." His voice cracked. "She'll take them. She'll kill them all."

"No," Lake said. Her insides twisted and squirmed like the tar in the box.

The boy's expression shifted at the plea in her voice. He suddenly looked uncertain. His grip loosened on the make-shift club.

"You have it wrong," Lake said. How was she supposed to explain it?

And wasn't it true?

I take people away. They never come back.

I take them to a dying ship where we wait to return to what might be a dead planet.

Willow appeared in the doorway, her face streaked with ash. She pointed silently at the sky, her expression taut. Lake looked up.

Thick black smoke.

In the distance, flames crackled.

We have to go. Now.

The boy saw Willow in the doorway, and his eyes went the same color as the sky overhead. "I knew it." He turned back to Lake. "You *are* her."

Lake looked down at the tar, a thicker mass of it than she'd ever seen. A stockpile, to defend the Battery against *her*.

She couldn't let him deliver it to the Battery.

But he was her best chance for finding the way there.

"Yes, I'm the one you've been waiting for," she said. "Take me to the Battery."

13

LAKE

"Willow, find some rope," Lake said. "We need it to haul the tar."

Willow dashed out of the supply room, and Lake felt better having her far from a nervous guy wielding a jagged tree branch.

Lake nodded at his branch-club. "That's no match for this tar. Leave it here."

She hoped he wouldn't call her bluff. No way she'd use the tar on him.

Taren paced near the door, squinting at the tar and the boy in turn. "Are you sure about this?" he asked Lake.

No. "We need to get to the Battery."

Willow returned with a coil of cord, the kind you'd use for tying camping gear to a car roof. As soon as Lake started wrapping it around the lead box, the boy dropped his weapon. He backed up against the wall and watched the tar roil in the box and finally said, "I'll probably get a reward for taking you there."

"Will you?" Lake pulled the cord taut, left a long lead. She spotted his name stitched on his jacket. "Good for you, Ajay. Can I call you Ajay? It's stitched on your jacket."

He looked down, as if he needed proof. "That doesn't mean it's my name."

"Okay, but can I call you that?" She was pretty sure he was just being cagey. "How many people are in the Battery?"

He narrowed his eyes. "We're just trying to get by. Wait out this mess." He lifted his gaze to the molten sky.

Speaking of. Got to get going.

"So, like, forty people?" Lake tried, eying the doorway, the falling ash, the red-sky tint to Ajay's skin. "Forty-five, maybe?"

"We have a whole community, we have rules," Ajay said, and Lake wondered if she should take that as a yes. "If someone needs more food from the cache, or tools, or whatever—"

"What cache?"

"Don't act like that's not why you want the Battery."

Why I want the Battery?

They think I want to take the place for myself?

"What's he talking about?" Taren asked, and Lake shot him a look that said, *You tell me.*

"Is that where all the stuff in this trading post came from?" Lake asked Ajay, wrapping the loose end of cord around her hand. "Some cache you found?"

Ajay watched Lake's careful work as if he were wishing she'd make a mistake and touch the tar. "You can't just come in and take everything for yourself."

"I've heard something about that—caches," Taren told Lake. "Tech bros buried them all over the place, for when they left their bunkers and had to start over. You heard about that underground bunker community in the missile silo in Kansas? It's like, Rich City, capital of New Doom. They have a pool and everything down there."

"We're not in Kansas," Lake reminded him.

"Toto," Willow added. The threat of death always brought out her worst humor.

"There are bunkers in California, too," Taren said. "And what's a millionaire going to do when he has to finally leave it?"

Open their hidden cache of survival supplies and restart their hegemony, apparently.

"We have a credit system, we have shops," Ajay cut in. "If someone needs a job done, we rotate workers, give them credits for their work."

I'm not trying to destroy your city. Lake stood and watched the ash piling at her feet. "That sounds nice," she said, and meant it. "It sounds fair." Her thoughts piled like ash.

A whole community, working together. Making a new life for themselves.

Maybe it wouldn't all be doom and ash when they returned home. Maybe they could figure out how to start over.

"Ready for a road trip?" Willow asked Ajay.

He grudgingly followed Willow and Taren out. Lake dragged the box after.

The main room was full of the snap and pop of the burning ghost-trees outside. The figments lazed at the tables with their cards.

"Careful," Taren said to Lake, watching the lead box slide too close to a cardplayer's foot.

"They're figments, Taren. It doesn't matter if the tar touches them." He looked unsure, so Lake added, "They'd disappear, that's it. They're not real people, you know?"

They didn't even look up when she said it, just went on examining their cards and breathing ash.

"I'll help," Willow said, and darted over to guide the box away from the table.

"No," Lake barked, and pushed her away.

Half a dozen pairs of eyes fell on her. Heat roiled toward her from the flames licking now at the tops of the walls.

Willow shrank back. "I know how to be careful around *tar*," she told Lake.

"I don't need help." Lake tugged the box, and it knocked into a table leg. She held her breath while she waited for the tar to stop sloshing. "Okay, I don't *want* help."

Willow pulled her jacket tight around herself. "Aren't you too late to worry about something bad happening to me?"

Lake's vision narrowed. She felt as if the molten sky were already pressing down on her, branding her with pain.

Someone put a steadying hand on her arm. "You okay?" Taren asked, and Lake realized he had come to stand next to her.

She took a breath to clear her thoughts. "I'm fine." She nudged the box with her foot and went on towing. It was easy—nothing was as heavy as her heart these days. She pushed a chair out of her path. "Open the door, Ajay."

Ajay balked. "It's too late. Don't you see the flames outside?"

They licked the bare roof beams, their glow making the rough trading post look like a little-visited corner of hell.

"I don't burn," Lake said dryly. "Open the door."

Ajay eyed the tar, then the door. He pushed the door open, marveled at what he saw beyond, and stepped through.

"Hurry, go," Lake said, and followed Taren and Willow through, dragging the box of tar behind her, sick with the feeling that she was towing her own doom.

They found themselves on a hillside under a cool blue sky. Feathery scrub, sea breeze. Lake guessed they were somewhere in the headlands just north of the city.

Taren stood before her, reading the clouds like a ship-bound sailor reads land on the horizon. Willow stood with him, jacket hanging off one shoulder, hair dancing in the breeze. Lake's lungs pumped salt-scrubbed air, her heartbeat as strong as the pound of distant waves against cliffs. *Only the rich and lucky survive,* she'd told Taren. But this was one of the few times she'd felt lucky since waking on the ship, standing here taking in brilliant sunlight and sculpted clouds. She'd heard once that a single cloud could weigh a million pounds, and she was suddenly struck now with the conviction that she would never earn such a heavy inheritance, that she had neither the strength nor the worthiness to receive such enormous beauty.

An itching regret fought for her attention. She ignored it a moment longer, in favor of clouds and Willow's glowing cheeks.

Then she had to face it: she shouldn't have let Ajay step through that door without anyone holding on to him.

She turned, searching for him.

She hated being right.

Ajay had found another stick, a long one perfect for tipping into the lead box and bringing forth a trembling clump of tar. Before Lake could react, Ajay touched the tar to the length of cord she held. She quickly dropped the cord. It fell to the ground in two pieces, her claim on the box severed.

"Back away from it," Ajay said, pointing the tarry stick at her.

"Fine," Lake said, stepping toward Willow and Taren. "I wasn't going to use it on you, though."

"No—just on everyone at the Battery," Ajay sneered.

"Not even them." Lake stared at the tar on his stick. "Are you going to use that on me?"

"I'm going to take you to the Battery. Isn't that what you wanted? I'm going to let them figure out what to do with you, so you can't hurt anyone else."

"I don't hurt people."

They looked at each other over the lifted stick. The only thing that moved was the tar squirming on the end of it, and the scrub shuffling in the wind. And Lake's heart, pumping madly inside her chest.

"Then what *do* you do with them?" Ajay finally asked.

I could show you. If I thought you were ready.

Was he ready?

"I'd never use tar on anyone," Lake said. "Where did you get all of it?"

"It gathers in places. All around San Francisco. It drifts in on the wind, from the blast site."

"You think it's from nuclear impact?" It wasn't fallout. Wasn't ash or dirt, either. It was something unique to the sim, clumps and strings of broken code.

Then again, maybe Ajay was right, in a way. The tar had always seemed to Lake to arise from horror and confusion, and what else had birthed those feelings but their memories of the warheads that had sowed the Earth with doom?

"They said on the news that nothing would grow for years." Ajay watched the tar squirm on the end of his club. Lake thought she could hear it sizzle against the cool air. "They said the soot from firestorms would hang in the air and block the sunlight and make everything die. And then one day, the skies would clear, and the world would get warmer, and things would grow."

All around them, the green of new growth mingled with the muted gold of wind-dried grass. Fennel shot up like feathers from the hide-back of the hillside. Deer tracks marked the dried mud along a trickling stream, the only bit of art Lake had seen in ages.

"But in the meantime," Ajay went on, "people would starve, world governments would collapse. Local governments would spring up, probably scary ones made of people who just like to hold guns."

Even seabirds were calling from overhead, or complaining to one another about the smell of smoke the four of them had brought with them. "Seems pretty nice here, though," Lake said.

Ajay squinted at the ruffled scrub and the water trickling along a muddy rut. He peered at thickets of wild fennel as if he were studying the face of a stranger.

Willow nudged Lake and pointed at a pair of young trees shading a tiny shack, just a hut of tied branches with a makeshift door—the door they'd come through minutes ago. Taren saw it too and shuffled his feet like he was thinking of escape.

But Lake couldn't help noticing how Ajay was reading the scenery, confusion mapped on his face. How he held his terrifying stick out to the side as if he could barely stand being near it.

"The Battery must be close," Lake said. "Must be a decent place to live with all of this right outside your door."

"I . . ." Ajay's shoulders drooped. "Sometimes I wonder why we're still living underground when . . ."

"Does anyone ever talk about leaving?" Lake asked. "Leaving for good?" *Do you want to leave? Come back with me to a failing ship, no grass or trees at all?*

Ajay shrugged. "Where else is there to go?"

Oh, I could tell you. But she'd learned early on—this couldn't be rushed.

"I've been all around," Ajay went on. "Collecting the tar. I've seen hellscapes you couldn't imagine—dead forests of gray trees, fields of skeletons half-buried in ash—"

Lake couldn't stand to hear more. "That's not the only thing waiting for us. There are other places to go."

Ajay looked from Lake to the green hillsides. He lifted his face to the sun and closed his eyes for the briefest moment. "No one seems to know how long we've been living in the Battery," he said. "We're down there, in the dark, barely knowing when it's day or night."

He wants to leave. He's ready. "So you *have* been thinking about leaving."

Taren tugged at the back of Lake's jacket. "Lake," he said, in a voice low enough that Ajay wouldn't hear. "We can't get to the Battery without him."

"It can't be far now," she said over her shoulder.

He caught her arm, pulled her closer so they could keep talking. "We don't know that."

Should she wait? Let Ajay take them right to the door? What if the Battery wasn't nearby at all and Ajay had only brought them here to corner them?

Chances to free people from the sim were so rare. But maybe Ajay could wait a little longer, could keep dealing with the tar and ash and uncertainty that had been his steady diet this long . . .

She shook her head. "No, that's not how this works. We don't keep people who want to go."

She waited for Taren to let go of her arm. He seemed to think that holding on would help her come to her senses.

His expression finally softened. He nodded in agreement and let go. But she caught the shadow in his gaze that said he thought they might regret this.

He probably wasn't wrong.

"I'm going to take the tar back to the Battery," Ajay said. "And then we'll be safe down there."

"No one's safe around tar." Lake watched the black stuff creep closer to Ajay's hand.

"We won't use it on *each other*."

"Who else will there be to use it on, when you're all locked in?"

Lake pored over Ajay's ash-speckled face, his ragged clothes, loose-tied sneakers. His jacket, one empty pocket gaping open, the other zipped shut and bulging.

There's always some object that shows what they're hung up on.

Lake eyed his zippered pocket, studied the circular bulge. A watch? "When did your watch stop? Or did it ever work at all?"

Ajay looked stricken. He shifted his tarry stick to his left hand so he could grasp his lumpy pocket with his right.

"Why don't you take a look at it?" Lake suggested. "Take it out of your pocket?"

The lines in Ajay's face deepened. "The zipper's stuck."

The stick he held had grown shorter this whole time, and the tar ate away at it still. In a minute, it'd reach Ajay's hand. "Did someone give you that watch?" Lake asked. "As a gift?"

Ajay's shoulders sagged. "I was supposed to wait for my cousin. One hour, and then we'd escape together. To . . . to a ship, I think."

He's remembering. Lake allowed hope to creep in.

"He gave me his watch and said he needed one hour to find his friends and tell them goodbye," Ajay went on. "But I got scared. I left without him."

Taren's shoulders jerked.

The tar, I know. It crept lower still, so close to Ajay's skin.

"We all left someone," Lake said, and Taren made that jerking movement again, so maybe it wasn't the tar upsetting him.

Willow just pulled at the ends of her jacket sleeves.

"Who did *you* leave?" Ajay asked, his voice hard, like he didn't believe her.

Lake closed her eyes, blocking out the sight of Willow shivering against the building wind. "Everyone. That's all we did—left people." She opened her eyes because she remembered, suddenly, some small bit of lukewarm hope: Ajay might have *someone* on the ship. A friend, maybe even his cousin. "What's your cousin's name?"

"Shawn. Shawn Singh." Ajay's fingers toyed with the zipper on his jacket. "He's not in the Battery. He's not *anywhere,* no one's seen him."

"I've seen him," Taren said.

Lake turned to him in surprise. She wondered if he were lying, but the excitement in his eyes said otherwise.

"I can't say we got off to a great start," Taren said. "But he's on the ship, he made it okay."

"He—what?"

"I've seen him," Taren said again. "He's waiting for you, I swear. You'll see."

"He's—?" Ajay frowned. But he was toying with the zipper again, and this time it budged. His fingers slipped through the opening.

Then he froze. Lake kept her gaze on the tar so near his skin.

"I keep having this weird thought," Ajay said. "Stupid, maybe. Did any of you ever play VR games in Paracosm?"

Lake and Taren exchanged glances. *Why yes,* Lake thought.

"Remember how people used to freak out and say that one day, we'd all get stuck inside VR and it'd be the end of the world?" Ajay cracked a smile. "One good thing about nuclear apocalypse—it proved them wrong."

Lake could hardly breathe, watching the tar creep. She gave Ajay a tight smile. "Sure did."

Ajay smiled back at her. He slipped his right hand into his pocket and drew out the watch.

Done.

Lake stepped toward him, pushed his left arm down so that he dropped the stick into the box of tar. His eyes flashed as if he suddenly realized what had almost happened, and he leaped away from the box like he'd been scalded.

But Lake didn't give him time to think about it. She turned him toward the shack under the trees. "Shawn's waiting for you."

She picked up a rock, walked to the door, and marked it with an X. Her way of letting him know: this door is special. It'll lead you out of here. She envisioned the ship waiting for him on the other side, and then opened the door for him.

Ajay glanced at the watch in his hand again. Lake wished she could take it and wind the time back, so Ajay would feel like the hour he'd been told to wait for his cousin had never passed.

At least Ajay would be with his cousin now. He stepped through the door and vanished.

The three of them were alone with the crate of squirming tar.

14

LAKE

Willow came running over the crest of the hill just as Lake turned to search for her. "I see it!" she called, her jacket flapping behind her. "The Battery!" She pointed back the way she'd come.

Lake and Taren exchanged hopeful glances. But then Taren said, "How will we get in without Ajay? At least if we had gone as his captives, he would have gotten us inside."

Lake thought of bad food on a broken ship. "I've had my fill of being a prisoner, personally."

Willow had caught her breath now. "Taren could make himself look like Ajay. They might let us all in if he tells them we're hoping for shelter."

Lake stared at her, stunned. Taren gaped. Then he said, "Did a computer program just come up with a good idea all on its own?"

Lake winced. But Willow just rolled her eyes and said, "Thanks, Taren. Anything *you'd* like to contribute?"

He still seemed ruffled, but in the end, he went to make a pocket where he could exchange his face for Ajay's. Near the shack nestled under the wind-stirred trees, he felt nearby for an invisible wall. Lake marveled at the way he pushed against the curtain of air. The hills beyond proved to be nothing but a backdrop, their edges caving as Taren pushed. In a moment, he had created a concave large enough to swallow him from sight.

The boy who reemerged looked nothing like the boy who had gone in. Taren pulled at the sleeves of his jacket—Ajay's jacket—and said, "Did I get it right?"

"Try a little more panic in your eyes," Willow said. "Ajay seemed committed to that emotion."

"You look great," Lake said. She hesitated, and then said, "Did you change the tattoo on your arm?"

Taren's brows contracted. "I'm wearing a jacket. No one will see it." He clasped his hand over the sleeved arm, as if to protect it.

"That's not what I meant. I was just thinking—before we go into the Battery, you should have a plan for remembering you're in the sim. Something to keep you grounded."

Taren glanced at Willow, Lake's *something that kept her grounded*, and his gaze clouded over. "Figments don't keep me grounded."

"I'm talking about your tattoo." Lake tried not to resent the way he'd looked at Willow. She moved close so she could roll up his sleeve. "You could change the pattern of the stars so that when you look at the tattoo, you'll know there's something not right about it."

Taren's arm went rigid under her hands. "I got this tattoo with my brother."

His injured tone made Lake back off. "Okay. It was just an idea."

"Whatever." Taren went on rolling his sleeve, a little stiffly. "That was a different lifetime, right?"

Lake wondered if she should apologize. But Taren was already turning back for the pocket he'd created. He disappeared into it and came out with his arm rigid at his side. Tattoo altered, Lake guessed. Taren gave it one quick glance, his face tight, like he was checking a wound.

Lake focused on using her foot to nudge the box of tar toward the pocket Taren had created. When she had it safely hidden, she turned back to find Taren squinting in thought.

"How are we going to know who in the Battery is a sleeper and who's a figment?" he asked. Lake found it weird to hear his voice coming from Ajay's mouth.

"It doesn't matter," Lake said, checking the toe of her boot for stray tar. "We just need the one dreamer. I'm guessing it'll be whoever's running the place."

"And after we figure out who the dreamer is?"

"We figure out how to wake the person. Honestly, they usually tell you what's keeping them in the sim. You just have to listen." She noticed the way he still held his tattooed arm rigid at his side and felt a stab of guilt for ever having suggested he change it. "Look around for an object that ties to whatever's bothering them."

Taren fixed his gaze at a spot just above her head. "That's what you did with me. Was I easy to figure out?"

Was it regret in his voice? Resentment? She couldn't understand what was going on with him.

"No," she said. "You were easy to care about. That's why I stuck with it."

His shoulders relaxed. But his gaze was still hard.

What did you expect? she asked herself. *Did you think he'd thank you for dragging him from the last place he felt safe?*

Her heart sank. *You think he came into the sim just to help? He's still bruised, and he's looking for something to heal him. Or . . .*

She remembered him at the overlook, his jaw clenched, his gaze fixed on the spot where she'd seen a figment jump the railing. A figment that had looked quite a bit like him, only older, more muscular.

Or something that'll bruise harder.

Lake had a bad habit of that herself, pressing on her own bruises.

"Are we going?" Willow asked, hands on her hips, impatient.

"Yeah," Taren answered.

Lake swallowed her nerves. "Wait, I should tell you."

Taren's shoulders went rigid again.

"It won't be easy to wake the dreamer here," Lake said. "Any dreamer who can create a pocket big enough to hold forty-plus sleepers has to be seriously deluded by the sim."

"You said we just had to look for an object. And listen to their sad story."

"Finding out why they won't leave the sim is one thing. Convincing them to go is another."

Taren blew out a breath. "You didn't feel like mentioning this earlier?"

"I was focused on finding the Battery earlier. One problem at a time, you know?"

Taren looked back at the pocket he'd created, the concave where Lake had stashed the tar. "We could find a way to get the dreamer out here, into the pocket I made. Then I could walk out that door over there"—he nodded at the shack under the trees—"to exit the sim. The pocket I made would close, the dreamer would wake, their pocket would close too. Then— everyone's out of the sim."

"Everyone who's inside the Battery, at least," Lake said. It wasn't a terrible idea. "Which might actually be everyone who's left in the sim."

"How are you going to get them to come out of the Battery and walk into the pocket you made?" Willow asked. "You have Girl Scout cookies or something?"

"Haven't figured that out yet," Taren said. "Maybe something will come to me inside the Battery."

Lake chewed her lip. "Maybe. We'll make it plan B." She started up the hillside, toward Willow. "Anything bad happens, just get out the nearest door, okay? We can regroup and come back later."

Behind her, Taren said, *"Later."* An edge to his voice.

Lake turned to give him a questioning look.

"With the state the ship is in," he said, "*later* isn't really an option."

Lake went on following Willow, trying not to feel the

weight of Taren's words. The thing was, she knew from experience one important truth: you can't rush it.

But she *also* knew what the fear in her gut told her: the chaos on the ship was only getting worse with each passing moment.

They had to wake the Battery's dreamer, and they had to do it now.

What if I can't do it? Even with Taren's help?

She wished Ransom were here. She wasn't sure how much help he could be, but at least when he was around, the scrabbling in her chest eased.

At least I'm not alone. She watched Willow's jacket flap behind her as she walked.

They crested the hill, and the hulking Battery came into view.

Thick concrete walls jutted from the hillside, splayed at an angle and barred by double gates. An enormous entry to an underground fortress, like a wide mouth into the earth. Shadowing the gates was a huge semicircle overhang of concrete like the palate of a monster.

If only places like this could actually have protected the people left behind.

"I know this place," Taren said. "Built to protect the coast during World War Two, but never even used. They finally filled it in to stop explorers from crawling down into it and trashing the place."

"Cool, great," Lake said, prodding him forward. The figures standing at the rusty gate had noticed them. "Things are different in the sim."

"*I* like history," Willow said, smiling at Taren.

His attention was only on the figures dwarfed by the Battery's entrance. "What if I'm supposed to know a secret handshake?"

"Tell them you forgot to wash your hands?" Willow suggested.

"Great, thanks." Taren edged out ahead, hands shoved in his jacket pockets, and lifted his head in greeting.

The two figures didn't respond. They leaned against the gate, bored by wind and sun and visitors alike.

"You know these guys?" the taller one said to the other, a girl with taut biceps and boots big enough to stamp small trees out of existence.

The boots-and-biceps girl watched Taren shuffle to a stop a good distance from the gate. She glanced at Lake and Willow while Lake held her breath. "Yeah, it's Ajay." She nodded at Taren. "Aren't you supposed to have something with you, Ajay?"

The tar. They knew Ajay was supposed to deliver it to the Battery.

Willow threw Lake a worried look. Lake tried to look unruffled.

"Supposed to," Taren said. "There's a whole story."

"Oh, good." The girl crossed one huge boot over the other, getting comfortable. "I like stories."

Taren hesitated. "Mind letting us inside first? It's been, you know, a long day." He didn't even have to try to sound exhausted.

"*You* can come in," the girl said. "I don't recognize the other two." She turned and reached through the bars of the rusted gate and pulled a long metal bar through, then cocked her arm like she was ready to start swinging.

Taren scrambled back, shielding Lake and Willow behind him. "Whoa, hey. These are friends of mine. They're just looking for shelter."

The girl hefted the rusted bar. Lake wondered what it would be like to get bashed in a simulation. The tightness in her chest told her she didn't want to find out.

"You're vouching for them?" the girl asked, holding the bar ready to swing on the off chance he might say no.

Taren held his hands high to fend off a blow. "Yes, I'm vouching for them!"

The other guard moved to haul open the gate. "Don't mind her, she's just messing with you." He scowled at his partner. "You didn't pull that on the guy who came in earlier."

The girl rolled her eyes. "You always get jealous if I don't threaten someone's life."

"You gave him a pretty warm welcome," the boy-guard said sourly.

"We're not the first ones to arrive today?" Lake asked.

The boy-guard was still moping. "Like, asphalt-in-sunlight warm."

The girl gestured with her rusted bar, waving them through. Taren passed with the stiffness of someone anticipating a blow. Lake held Willow's hand and they walked through together.

Just inside the entrance was a vertical shaft tinged with orange light. The throat of a beast. Taren went down first. His wide eyes stayed fixed on Lake until he passed the edge and she could see him no more. Willow went next. Then Lake.

The voices of the two guards followed her down the shaft. "That guy who came before them didn't even have anyone to vouch for him."

At the bottom of the shaft was a concrete tunnel lit by bracketed torches. And then—

The tunnel opened, and a city bloomed before them.

Blocky buildings jutted from the cavern walls, their walls pocked, corners rough as if unfinished. Their flat roofs splayed under the sunlight struggling through a narrow crevice overhead. Dozens of people milled through the place, boys with uneven stubble along their jaws, and girls with dirt streaked over their muscled arms. They carried crates of jerky and Red Vines and Coke, or armloads of blankets and nylon jackets. Loose stones clattered under their feet. More tumbled from windowsills and from steps that emerged from the ground even as Lake watched, and from doorways that slowly etched themselves into existence.

Lake's insides turned to water. *I can't wake this dreamer. Whoever it is is in too deep.*

She turned to Taren, but he seemed lost in confusion, watching the buildings inch into existence, the sleepers pass in and out of shadow. "How many of them do you think are figments?" he asked Lake.

She shook her head. She didn't know. It didn't matter. Why was he so fixated on figments? Was it because of Willow—or could it have something to do with the figment Lake had spotted at the overlook?

But the next moment, she forgot all about it. Because she realized who had arrived at the Battery earlier that day. She *saw* him. Sitting at a makeshift table of stacked crates, just visible through a carved window, the torchlight burnishing his face along the planes she had so recently traced with her fingertips—

Ransom.

Lake stepped closer, telling herself that she was mistaken, that Ransom couldn't have found his way here.

But there he was, hunched over a table of stacked crates, flanked by two sleepers, the light lending fire to his troubled gaze.

"He didn't have anyone to vouch for him," she murmured.

Willow darted to her side. "Is that Ransom? What's he doing here?"

Ransom looked up at the sound of his name. A flash of recognition in his eyes. Then, back to stony misery.

What would happen to him if she closed this pocket of the sim while he was inside it? He'd never been able to leave the sim before. He wouldn't wake up on the ship like any other sleeper. Would it be like using tar on him—would he go into shock?

"He has to leave," Willow said, "before we close the pocket."

Ransom locked his gaze on Lake's and moved his head just barely side to side. A warning.

"He can't," Lake said. "He's their prisoner."

15

TAREN

Taren darted after Lake and Willow, into a shadowed alcove. The pattering of falling dust and rubble filled the space as the alcove slowly deepened into a shallow hallway.

"What's wrong?" Taren asked.

"We saw someone we know," Willow said. "They're holding him prisoner."

Taren looked to Lake. The hallway went on widening behind her, so that it seemed she was being swallowed by shadow and stone. "We have to get him out of here," she said, "before we try to close the pocket."

What? Taren had come to wake the dreamer. This was only a distraction. And anyway, it didn't make sense. "He's someone you know from the ship?"

"From the sim," Lake said. "He's a sleeper."

"The *deepest* sleeper," Willow said.

Taren dodged a fall of dust. "What does that mean?"

"He knows he's in a simulation," Lake explained, "but he still can't leave it, no matter how hard he tries."

That didn't really clear things up. *I just want to get on with finding the dreamer.*

"If we close the pocket while he's inside," Lake went on, "I don't know what'll happen to him."

"He knows he's in a simulation but he can't get out?" Taren said. "That doesn't make sense. Are you sure there isn't something else going on with him?"

Lake rubbed a hand over her face. Behind her head, an intricate pattern etched itself into the rock wall of the hallway. "We just need to get him out of here."

There's something she isn't telling me.

As usual.

"What's he even doing here?" Taren asked. "He wanted to join the Battery club?"

"Ransom's more of a loner," Willow said. "He's a bit of a grouch."

Taren shook his head. "I don't get it—he just showed up here for no reason?"

"I don't know why he's here," Lake said, an edge to her voice. "We just have to get him out."

Taren gritted his teeth. He didn't understand any of this. But Lake was hunched with misery, the gloom of the hallway a dark cloak around her.

He took a deep breath. "I'll go tell his guards I vouch for him. Maybe they know Ajay."

Lake straightened, a hopeful glow in her eyes. It was almost enough to counter Taren's frustration. Almost. "His name's Ransom," she said.

Taren nodded. Then he left the hallway before he could change his mind.

Ransom looked up as Taren stepped into the doorway. The two guards went on balancing carved-stone dominos on a table of stacked crates.

"Looks like my friend showed up before I could get here," Taren said to the guards, nodding at Ransom. "Sorry about the mix-up. I can vouch for him."

Ransom stared, the torchlight gleaming in his eyes.

Just play along. Taren tried to say it with a look.

One of the guards glanced up, gave Taren a smirk. "It's a little late for that."

"He was asking a lot of *interesting* questions," the other guard said. "I think we're past vouching."

"So he's curious about his new hangout." Taren forced a smile that neither guard returned. "Who wouldn't be?"

The first guard plunked down another domino. "We're taking him to Eden as soon as we finish our game."

Eden—is she the leader of this place? The heavy look Ransom gave him confirmed his guess.

That means she's the dreamer.

"I can take him to Eden," Taren said. "I'm supposed to report to her on a job she sent me to do."

"You mean collecting tar?" one of the guards said. "Where is it?"

Ransom's shoulders jerked. His expression flooded with dread.

Yeah, I brought tar here. But don't worry, it's hidden.

"That's what I have to report to her about," Taren told the guard.

The mention of tar had clearly made the other guard nervous. He almost upended the crate-table in his attempt to place his next domino. "We shouldn't have that stuff here," he said. "Hasn't anyone else seen what it does?"

Ransom leaned back on the crate serving as a stool. The shadows on his face shifted. "I've seen. If there's tar here, this place isn't safe."

The first guard waved a hand toward Taren. "Fine, just take him. Let us get on with our game."

Ransom hesitated, but Taren took his arm and pulled him up. He didn't want to give the guards a chance to change their minds. "So Eden's just . . . ?" *Where, exactly?*

The guard pointed in the direction of a narrow passageway without looking up from his game. "Her usual place."

"Usual," Taren echoed. "Right."

He led Ransom back to the hallway where Lake and Willow were waiting. Lake immediately pulled Ransom close in a way that made Taren look away. Willow caught his eye and grimaced, but sharing a moment with a figment only made Taren *more* uncomfortable.

Lake pushed Ransom away now, her expression turning stern. "What are you doing here?"

"I wanted to help." Ransom slumped against the wall. "But I think I'm just screwing things up."

"Actually . . ." Taren said, and earned a glare from Lake.

"How did you even get here?" Lake asked Ransom.

"I followed someone," he said. "I didn't even know if it would work. Guess the sim's being kind to me today." He shifted away from the rubble trickling down the wall next to him.

"It's never kind," Taren said. "Even the good parts are only a trick."

"You don't mean that," Willow said, looking put out.

Lake cut in. "We need to get you out of here," she said to Ransom.

Taren shifted, accidentally scraped his elbow on newly cut rock. "They're expecting me to take him to the leader of this place. If he disappears, someone's going to get suspicious."

Lake glared at him again. "Then we better get him out of here before they have time to get suspicious."

"That's what I'm saying." Taren held out his palms in defense. "You get him out of here while I go talk to the leader. She's expecting me—or Ajay, anyway."

"You want to try to wake the dreamer alone?" Lake scoffed. "You're still new at this, there's no way you can do it on your own."

Taren bristled. His brother's face flashed through his mind, wearing that dismissive smirk. "*You think* you *can fix anything?*"

"I woke the sleepers at the house," Taren pointed out. *In the same pocket where* you *almost got trapped.*

"This is going to be a *lot* harder," Lake said.

Taren knew Lake was only anxious about her boyfriend, but he couldn't help resenting her sharp tone. "I know that."

"Don't worry about me," Ransom cut in. "I can get myself out."

"How?" Lake asked.

"The guards at the gate are friendlier than the ones down here," he said.

"He's going to flirt," Willow translated.

Ransom ignored her. "You go talk to Eden, I'll get out on my own," he told Lake. He pulled her close before she could protest what he'd said. "I promise I'll turn up again somewhere else."

Lake relaxed in his arms like Taren had never seen her do. For just that moment, her anxiety seemed to relent. Then she pulled free, and all her electric energy was back.

She angled herself to peer out of the hallway. The light revealed her to be half-coated in dust, as if the Battery were turning her into another etching. "Hurry," she told Ransom, "while no one's looking."

Ransom pressed her hand as he slid past her. "I found out something that might help you: the leader of this place had a sister."

"What?" Lake was still focused on keeping watch.

"She begged for her sister to come along on the ship," Ransom said, "but her sister was over eighteen, so they wouldn't let her come. Maybe that information will help you."

Lake brushed dust from his hair. "Maybe so. Thank you."

Ransom slipped out of the hallway, and Lake stood for a long moment, watching him go.

Taren tried to squash his impatience. "We should go."

"I know." She kept her gaze focused on the place where Ransom must have vanished through the buildings by now.

She thinks I can't manage on my own. But she's *the one who keeps forgetting we don't have time to waste.*

He heard a low voice coming from the end of the hallway, and he spun to peer into the darkness. *Taren,* it said.

A familiar voice: Gray's.

It wasn't coming from the hallway. It was inside his own mind.

The ship is breaking down, the voice said.

I know, Taren told Gray silently.

The voice came again: *If I were on that ship, I'd clear out the sim so fast. I'd do whatever it took.*

Taren squirmed. What would it take?

It didn't matter. He had only this one chance.

I will too. I'll do whatever it takes.

16

LAKE

Taren led the way through a narrow passage between looming rock-buildings. Lake's adrenaline was so high she hardly registered the uneven ground beneath her feet, the rough-cut walls of the narrowing buildings. "Do you think Ransom's out?" she asked.

"He said he could manage," Taren reminded her.

"He's probably already back in his pub," Willow said, "building Coit Tower out of toothpicks."

The passageway opened into a wide cavern with other narrow alleys leading away from it.

Sunlight streamed through an opening in the vaulted ceiling. It illuminated walls painted with red mud and glinting with the jagged edges of embedded stones. At the edge of the light, a teenage girl sat on a stone outcropping like a weathered throne, flanked by half a dozen shadowy figures.

Eden, the dreamer.

She wore a faded school uniform, odd clothing for a queen,

and a crown of dried leaves. "We've been waiting for you," she said to Taren, her voice slow as the water trickling down the cavern walls.

Lake quailed. But then she remembered: Eden had sent Ajay on an errand. Now she expected a report.

"I don't have the tar," Taren said. "It . . . it was stolen."

"Stolen?" Eden sounded more intrigued than alarmed.

A bad sign.

"These two tried to help me," Taren said, gesturing to Lake and Willow on either side of him. "They're looking for shelter. I can vouch—"

Eden waved a hand, and Taren stopped speaking. "These two—where did they come from?"

Lake glanced at Willow, who seemed transfixed by the red sludge pooling at the base of the walls. "We came from an empty neighborhood," Lake said. "A ghost town."

Eden skewered Willow with her gaze. "And is this your sister?"

Lake kept quiet, sure Eden would know if she were lying.

One of the soldiers flanking Eden's makeshift throne approached, and she let him speak into her ear. Taren shot Lake a worried look.

Eden gestured to someone in the shadows, and the girl-guard from the gate stepped from the mouth of a passageway, using her metal bar to prod along a prisoner.

Ransom.

Lake bit back a cry. He hadn't gotten out. Her gut had told her he wouldn't, and her gut had been right.

He gave her an apologetic look that melted her. Even when

he was coated with dust and weary with disappointment, she wished she could hold him. *You dummy, you should've never come here.*

Eden's voice broke through her thoughts. "And who is this boy?"

Taren cleared his throat, so obviously nervous that it pained Lake. "I don't know. I met him here." He glanced at Lake. What could they say to get Ransom out?

The girl-guard tipped her head to one side. "I heard you tried to vouch for him," she told Taren.

"He seems harmless," Taren said. "I think he was just curious about this place."

Eden raised her brows. "He must not have liked what he learned. He tried to leave."

"Why not let him go?" Taren said.

Eden stared coolly at Taren, clearly unused to being told what to do.

We have to think of something to turn this around.

Ransom lifted his head, signaling to Lake. He threw his glance toward Eden and mouthed, *Her sister.* Lake followed his gaze to the locket Eden wore, a globe of tarnished gold. She'd seen Eden's hand flutter to the tiny globe when she'd said the word *sister* a moment ago. Ransom was trying to tell her to get Eden talking so Lake could find a way to wake her from the sim.

But what about you? Lake wanted to ask Ransom. *I can't wake Eden until I get you out of here.*

If she woke Eden and closed the Battery with Ransom inside . . .

What will happen to you, Ransom? Will you go into shock? Will you survive?

Taren nudged his shoe against Lake's, prodding her to speak. "If you don't have enough supplies for us all," Lake said to Eden, "then we can leave."

Taren jerked his head around to look at her, stunned. Obviously, that wasn't what he'd had in mind. He wanted her to wake Eden.

We'll have to come back and try later.

"We have plenty of supplies," Eden said, scowling. "For those who are welcome here."

"She only wants to take care of her *sister*," Ransom cut in, and alarm flared through Lake again.

Please, Ransom, I'm trying to keep you safe.

The iron in Eden's eyes softened. "I tried too, to take care of my sister. But she wasn't chosen to survive."

Guilt stabbed at Lake. Everyone on the ship had been chosen over someone else.

Even Lake.

And it didn't make sense—none of them deserved what they'd been given. Not the survivors on the ship, and not the ones who'd been left behind.

"Now *I* choose who survives," Eden said.

Lake shivered.

She and Eden weren't so different. Eden had lost her sister and created a stronghold where she'd never again be powerless. Lake had lost her sister and set herself to tearing down strongholds like Eden's.

Eden deserves to wake. She deserves to survive.

But then, didn't Ransom deserve the same thing?

"You choose," Lake said to Eden, agreeing. "You choose who comes to the Battery, and who leaves. You can let us go. We won't ask for your supplies."

Next to her, Taren was shaking his head. He gave Lake a questioning look.

We can try again later. But she knew what Taren would say to that: *There is no later. The ship is failing now.*

"I can vouch for them," he tried again, putting his hand on Willow's shoulder and then pulling back again, as if remembering she was only a figment. "They tried to help me deliver tar, but we were attacked."

Eden smiled. Her eyes gleamed. "Oh, I know about the tar."

Lake's nerves lit up. Something about Eden's catlike smile.

"Do you know who this girl is?" Eden asked, leaning forward to catch Taren's full attention. "Who you're so eager to vouch for? I do."

Taren clutched Lake's hand.

"A girl who can look like anything," Eden said. "Who often travels with her younger sister."

Lake kept herself from looking over at Willow. *But Eden already knows. She guessed it, just like Ajay did.*

"Around here, we call her the Angel," Eden said.

The boys leaning against the walls stood straighter, shoulders bunching.

Eden sat taller on her misshapen throne, a queen about to pronounce judgment. "The Angel of Death."

Lake trembled. "We only came here to—"

"When *you* show up," Eden cut in, "people disappear."

The boys glowered at her. The red mud covering the walls, glowing in the light, tinted their skin so that they seemed bathed in resentment.

"What do you want?" Lake asked Eden. "You want us to leave? We'll leave."

Eden's smile was gone. "I know where you came from. I know why you want to be rid of us."

She knows? She remembers about the ship?

"You guard the location of a lost world," Eden said.

Lake stared at Eden, stunned. "A lost world?"

Blue trees growing next to a river.

"She means the ship," Taren said under his breath. "She's ready."

Lake frowned. *I don't think that's what she means at all.*

And Lake had another idea. Plan B.

"I'll show you the entrance to the lost world." *The pocket Taren made not far from the Battery gates.* "If you let him go." She pointed at Ransom.

Eden's eyes gleamed. "Done." She gestured to her soldiers and they moved toward Ransom.

"Lake," Ransom said, his voice uncertain. "What . . . ?"

Just trust me. She kept her gaze on him as a couple of soldiers pulled him toward an alleyway.

"Well?" Eden prompted.

Lake watched Ransom vanish through the mouth of the alley and tried to feel relief. *He'll get out, at least.*

Will we?

"It's not far," Lake told Eden, speaking slowly, trying to give Ransom time to get out of the Battery.

"You'll show me," Eden said, rising from her stone mount.

"It's here in these hills," Lake said, still stalling. "Near a grove of new trees."

Eden froze. She sank back onto her throne. "A grove of new trees," she echoed.

Anxiety knifed through Lake.

"You would lead me *there*?" Eden asked.

Lake looked to Taren, but he seemed just as confused as she was. "We'll take you to the lost world," Lake told Eden. But Lake could sense it—*Eden suspects something's off.*

A poisoned smile spread slowly across Eden's face. Lake knew then: she'd failed. She wasn't going to wake Eden. She wasn't going to lead her out to the pocket Taren had created. This wasn't working at all.

Lake had wanted to save Ransom, and she thought she had probably managed that.

But at the cost of saving all the sleepers in the Battery.

She looked at Taren. *I'm sorry,* she mouthed.

He frowned, confused. He was gripping her hand hard, just as nervous as she was about Eden's fuming silence.

But now his grip loosened, and understanding came into his eyes. He knew Lake had been stalling and that they'd lost their chance to wake Eden.

Eden's voice rang off the cavern walls: "You would lead me to the same grove of trees next to where you hid *this*?" She gestured to someone in the shadows, and the girl-guard from the gate used her metal rod to push a box into the shaft of sunlight.

Inside the box, the tar was a mass of shadows.

"My soldiers saw you hide this in the hills," Eden said.

Lake went hot all over. Next to her, Taren shook like he remembered his legs had been mostly immobile for decades.

"You stole our tar," Eden said, "and brought it here to use against us."

"No." Lake's voice shook. "I came to help you. Please, the tar is dangerous. You have to get rid of it."

Eden snapped her fingers. The girl who had dragged in the box of tar now dipped her metal rod into the dark mass. She held it out, her stare fixed on the wriggling nothingness clinging to the end of it.

"Please," Lake said, shifting her gaze from the tar to Eden. "You don't understand what this is."

Eden stepped forward. "I know where it came from: blown out of hell by a nuclear weapon."

She nodded to the girl, who stepped toward Lake, holding her weapon out before her.

"Listen to me," Lake said, backing away from the tarred rod, pulling Taren with her. "I'm not some Angel of Death."

Eden watched, eyes like glassy stones. "Whatever death-touch you possess has no reach like this does."

A thrill went through Lake's heart at the sight of the tar coming toward her, and of Eden standing in triumph. *You and I*, Lake wanted to say to her, *we're both doing what we have to do.*

"Wait," Taren said, his voice so sharp it rang against the cavern walls in the same way Eden's had. "Listen to me, Eden. You've been living underground for months now. You made a city beneath a battery."

Eden waited, transfixed by the same forceful tone that had Lake waiting for Taren to say more.

"But how can that be?" Taren went on. "This place was filled in ages ago. They made it impossible to get inside."

Lake shot Taren an alarmed look. What was he doing?

"And now there's a whole city under here?" Taren said. "Carved out of rock? Using—what tools?"

Eden swayed, reached out a hand as though to steady herself. The hard planes of her face softened, her confidence slipping.

"And where did all of the stuff come from?" Taren pressed. "All the food and cans and bottles? You think that stuff would survive nuclear winter?"

"Taren," Lake said. She knew what he was doing now, why his gaze was roving the floor, the walls. "Stop."

"We found a cache," Eden said, but her face was lined with uncertainty.

"Even in a cache, food doesn't last forever. Especially not the kind of food I've seen in your city. And what's a city without food?" His head jerked in a way that told Lake he'd found what he was looking for. She followed his gaze to where a drop of tar trickled over Eden's stone mount. As they watched, another drop fell onto the stone from the opening in the ceiling above, and then a slurry, thick as the mud dripping down the walls.

"You think you can keep all these people safe?" Taren stepped toward Eden, shoulders high like an animal cornering its prey. "That's not what you're doing at all. You drew all these people down here where there's nothing to eat, no air, no life. You've trapped them."

Eden let out a small noise, a shrill note of guilt.

"They're going to die down here, and it's all *your* fault."

Taren pounced. He shoved Eden backward, toward the stone seat, coated now in the tar that dripped from above.

But Eden's soldiers were quick. They dove for her, and one of them managed to throw her to the ground just before the soldier himself fell back against the tarry stone.

The boy cried out. The tarry nothingness bubbled and spread, eclipsing cheek, wide eye, gaping mouth. The next moment it was a veil, and then a cloak, and then a burial shroud—

And then the boy-soldier was gone.

Lake gaped, sick and shaking.

Taren stood just as still, his face reflecting the shock and horror that had shown on the boy-soldier's face just a moment earlier.

Then the soldiers burst into motion, scrambling from the shadows.

Taren snapped into action before Lake could think what to do. He tore the metal rod from the hand of the girl-guard, who had gone stiff with shock. He turned and swung the rod, painting tar over the arm of the nearest soldier.

Lake found her voice. "Taren, stop! They're not figments!"

But he was trapped in the middle of the brawl now, battered by sticks and wooden slats, and he could only swing the metal rod, flinging tar at the soldiers.

One by one, they fell, shrieking as they bubbled out of existence.

And Taren didn't stop. He pushed into the fight, swinging the rod, painting tar over every arm and back and shoulder. Moving with a fury that said he'd waited too long for this, that he resented every person who held him captive—not only in this cavern, but in the crumbling existence he found himself fated to.

Lake pulled Willow away from the fray, toward a narrow alleyway. "The tar," Willow said, turning back for the box.

She was right—they couldn't leave the box of tar. It sat on the stone floor, guarded from the soldiers by Taren's attacks. Lake seized it by its cord-wrapping. Then she turned back for the alleyway, praying the tar wouldn't jostle over the sides and onto her bare hands.

Something caught her eye that made her stop in her tracks.

The rivulets dripping down the cavern walls were water no longer. They were tar, and where they tracked, they left wide cracks in the stone.

And through the stone—

Muted sunlight.

Lake stepped closer. She set the box at her feet while chaos reigned behind her. She pressed her hands against the walls, and the cracks widened under her fingertips, the stone falling away as dust.

A rush of cool air. A purple glow of light.

All around, shouts of horror and confusion rang against the walls.

"Come on, Willow," Lake said, knocking more stone away with the heels of her hands.

"Lake?" Willow said, her voice full of uncertainty as she peered through the crumbling wall.

But they needed to escape.

So Lake grabbed Willow's hand and pulled her through.

17

TAREN

Taren ran through the narrow passageways of the underground city, his ears full of the scrape of his shoes over rubble, the echoing clang of the metal rod he had dropped. His hands were stiff claws as he climbed the ladder, gasping and desperate for air not tainted by the smell of wet stone and sweat. *Don't think about their faces. Don't think about them gasping at the tar creeping over their skin . . .*

Somehow, he was at the hut under the trees. He wrenched the door open and stepped through to anywhere, anywhere at all—

A world of cold fog. Asphalt beneath his feet. Steel beams overhead, the orange-red of the Golden Gate Bridge. The paint was peeling, the metal beneath rusted, so that the beams looked scabbed.

Taren breathed in cool air, breathed out warm fog.

He was on the bridge, far from the Battery.

And Lake—where was she?

He thought he'd seen her step through a doorway in the cavern where there should have been no doorway. It didn't make sense. He was losing it. He couldn't stop shaking in the cold, but he felt hot all over. He tore off his jacket. The black stars tattooed on his forearm didn't look right, and it made him feel sicker than ever.

Don't look at it.

He looked around instead. At the tower of the bridge rising into oblivion. At the metal railing, and the glimpses of flat seawater below, gray like concrete.

But he couldn't stop thinking about the tattoo. He clutched his arm, covering the stars with his palm. He'd changed them, rearranged the constellation that was meant to forever tie him to his brother.

What did I do?

Something inside him had changed too.

He turned away from the railing, wishing his brother were there to help him. *We were trapped. There were so many of them. I had to get us out.* Gray would understand.

A shadow emerged from the fog.

Taren stared, rooted to the spot.

The fog thinned. The shadow turned to form.

"Gray?" Taren's heart thudded. His brother was here. A *figment* of his brother, but even so, he could help Taren make sense of things. Taren walked toward him, slowly at first, trying to read Gray's furrowed brow and rigid shoulders. Then more quickly, as if compelled by the weight that had settled over him like the cold fog. He landed his shoulder under Gray's and let his brother sling an arm around his neck.

"What's going on?" Gray asked, almost laughing. He took Taren by the shoulders and tried to look into his downturned face.

"I went to the Battery," Taren said. "I almost didn't get out."

"The Battery," Gray echoed. "Waking sleepers?"

Taren hesitated. Nodded.

Were the sleepers waking? Or were they dying in their stasis beds even now, succumbing to the shock of their violent ejection from the sim?

"Why feel bad about that?" Gray asked. "It's the only way you'll ever get home."

Taren's chest loosened. *Maybe so.*

"You woke them all?" Gray asked, his hands heavy on Taren's shoulders.

"No. Not all." The sweat on the back of Taren's neck felt as if it were turning to ice. He hadn't gotten to the dreamer, Eden. The one he most needed to wake.

Gray let go of Taren's shoulders. Taren looked up to find disappointment etched on brother's face.

"I couldn't," Taren explained. "I tried, but . . ." *I failed.*

Failed. He read the word in Gray's frown.

"You can't go home until you wake them all," Gray said.

"I know." Taren wished Gray would put a hand on his shoulder again.

But Gray was looking at Taren's arm. He grabbed it and scrutinized the tattooed stars with confusion, and then disgust.

"I had to change it," Taren said quickly. "So I wouldn't forget where I was. I didn't want to get trapped."

The stars tattooed on Gray's own arm were deep, inky black. Immutable. "But you aren't going to forget me, are you? Or Mom and Dad?"

"No," Taren croaked. "How could I?"

Gray let go of his arm with a skeptical sigh. He peered up at the bridge towers looming over them. "I can never go home. Never again."

Taren squeezed his eyes shut. He couldn't think about it.

"At least *you* have a chance at getting home," Gray went on.

The chill of the fog relented a little. Taren opened his eyes, hopeful for more warmth from Gray.

But Gray frowned. "And what are you doing with that chance? Wasting it." He shook his head. "Maybe you don't deserve it."

Taren's stomach dropped.

"You survived and I didn't." Gray glowered at him. "Do you think that makes any sense?"

Gray, genius mechanic.

And what am I? Why should I survive if he didn't?

"You don't deserve it," Gray said. "Not after what you've done."

Dread seeped into Taren's bones. "I attacked those sleepers." *How did Gray know?*

His brother's eyes held no sympathy anymore, only accusation.

But this was not his brother. This was a stolen face, and lines of code.

"I had to wake them," Taren said through clenched teeth. "*You're* the one who told me to do whatever it took."

"You don't deserve it," Gray said again. "Not after what you've done."

Taren turned his back, escaping from the judgment in the figment's gaze. "I don't want to talk to you anymore."

But a second figment appeared in front of him. A twin of Gray. Same accusing stare, same menacing growl: "You think you *deserve* to survive?"

Taren stumbled back. He whipped around to find the first figment still standing there. "What did you do?" it asked.

"I did what I had to," Taren shot out. "I woke the sleepers. I fought the machine that keeps us trapped."

He turned away, trying again to escape. But now a third figment appeared as if born from the fog, its clothes wet, its face traced with dripping water.

Like the water that had dripped down the cavern walls.

Dripped, and turned to tar.

The third figment stared at Taren in horror, its eyes wide. "What did you do?"

Taren raked his fingers over his own fog-wet arms, sick with guilt. "I took a spot on a ship, just like you did. And I survived." He wished the fog would swallow him. It draped itself over his skin like a creature with a cold embrace. "You didn't survive and I did—it's the worst thing I've ever done."

Misery pounded in his chest like a second heartbeat.

"You survived," the dripping figment said. "And now you must pay for it."

Taren shook his head. "You don't know anything." *How could I ever pay for something like that?* "You're not real. You don't understand what it's like—"

"You think you *deserve* to survive?"

The words came from the figment to his left this time. Taren turned and gave it a sharp shove. "Stop saying that."

"What did you do?" asked the figment to his right.

Taren turned again, lashed out with another shove. "Stop."

The third figment said, "You survived. And now you must pay."

"*Stop.*" The word erupted from Taren as he turned toward the Gray who had last spoken. He surged forward to shove the figment with more strength than he knew his shaking body could muster.

The figment jerked back. Too late, Taren realized that it had been standing at the railing.

It tumbled over, its face a mask of shock.

Taren's heart exploded in his chest. The rest of him turned to stone as he watched the figment fall past the railing, nothing to stop it from hitting the concrete-hard water below. One minute there, the next minute swallowed by fog.

For a moment, Taren couldn't move or think or even breathe. Then, the other two figments flew to the railing as if they could stop what had already happened.

Taren turned toward the base of the bridge tower that loomed over him. His breath came in searing gasps as he found a handle and yanked open the utility door and stepped into what he hoped would be the cradle of his stasis bed.

He woke to the hum of machines. His chest heaved as he pushed away the plastic shell over his bed and then got to his feet.

How easy to feel, in this distant place, that it had all been a bad dream.

That wasn't Gray. It wasn't anyone at all.

He made his breathing slow, his gut relax. He slid open the panel.

Beyond, a new nightmare: all the lights had died.

18

L A K E

The doorway led from the cavern into a dark forest. Deep shadows. Purple light. The leaves overhead were darker than any leaves Lake had ever seen, plum shades that cooled the blood boiling through her veins.

"Where are we?" Willow asked beside her.

Lake remembered what Ransom had told her: one day, she'd go so far into the sim that she'd never come back out.

She looked over her shoulder. She couldn't see the door into the Battery anymore.

Ahead: dense shadows, soft light.

"We can't go back to the Battery," Lake said, as if that were an answer to Willow's question. But it was true. The Battery was tar and death and horror. It was Taren, transformed into something she didn't understand. Something angry and fearful.

As if reading her thoughts, Willow said, "Taren attacked them."

"He thought they were figments," Lake said, and could almost admit to herself that she was lying. "He didn't think it mattered."

"They weren't figments."

"I know."

"He knew Eden wasn't—"

"He thought he had to wake her any way he could." Maybe he had been right. "And he didn't know, until he used it, what it would be like. Remember when he asked us the odds of someone surviving it?"

Willow walked in silence for a long moment. "But once he saw, he didn't stop."

Lake didn't have a reply for that.

She moved slowly, the lead box heavy in her arms, the tar roiling just inches from her skin. Every time she looked at it, she saw it coating the sleepers in the Battery, erasing them from the sim. *What did you do, Taren?* She shouldn't have taken him to the Battery. She'd seen that he wasn't ready, that something had been eating at him.

"We need a place to hide this," she said. She couldn't stand to look at it anymore, hated it being so close to her. And she didn't want anyone else to find it and use it on any more sleepers.

Willow darted forward. "Here." She knelt next to a tree whose trunk seemed to be shedding a layer of soft bark-skin. It split easily when she tugged, revealing harder bark beneath.

Lake eased the box to the ground, never taking her eyes from the squirming tar. She pushed the box under the tree's open jacket of bark, and then Willow let the bark fall over the box.

"Come on," Lake said, holding out her hand to help Willow up.

Willow just stared up at her for a long moment, her gaze clouded with the same shock Lake still felt. Then Lake leaned forward and grabbed Willow's hand, because if they stayed like this, they'd start to unravel, two more unjacketed trees.

They walked farther into the forest, away from the hidden cache of tar, following a trickling stream. In Lake's mind, images played over and over: tar like a sheath over crumpling bodies, Taren's pained grimace.

She remembered him asking how many of the Battery-dwellers were figments. But couldn't he see, hadn't he heard her calling out to him? They weren't figments. They were sleepers.

What did he do?

Wake the sleepers?

Or jolt them to their deaths?

Her lungs hardened again. She almost couldn't breathe at all.

Willow slipped her hand free of Lake's and walked ahead, drawn by something Lake couldn't see. "Come look," she called back.

The stream they'd been walking along had widened, and Lake heard what was up ahead before she saw it. The trees parted, and there was Willow at the top of a waterfall, at the edge of a precipice, like she had come to the world's end.

Lake stood next to her and marveled at what lay below.

A land of trees, blue in shadow. Or no—their leaves were dark, even in sunlight, like the trees Lake and Willow had just emerged from. In one direction, the forest gave way to golden tundra. In the other, to a dark, ice-capped ocean that seemed to swallow almost all light. And cutting through the middle: a river fed by the waterfall, so that the whole place seemed divided between day and night.

A lost world.

A strange place, and lovely. Born from a powerful imagination, the dream of someone deep in sim-sleep.

The sun on the horizon wasn't a sun but a glowing orb wedged into the dome of the sky. The trees below were not trees but ballooning umbrellas of leafy membrane. The world below had come from a dream so deep, Lake feared the dreamer would never wake.

"Who do you think made this place?" Willow asked. "It seems like what a person would make if they'd only ever heard someone describe the world and had never seen it for themselves."

The sun, an orb-like lamp. The ocean, a sheet of darkness. The river, a dividing line.

So strange. And yet . . .

Have I been here?

Willow gazed down at the landscape as if into the face of someone she thought she'd never see again. "They made it so beautiful."

Lake's heart went into her throat. Yes, it was beautiful.

Beautiful and vast and complex. So much more so than the Battery.

"This is what's killing the ship, isn't it?" Willow asked. "It's straining the sim so much it's shutting down the ship's systems."

And taking us with it.

Willow turned to her, backed by the wide, curving sky. "How are we going to close it?"

19

TAREN

Darkness had swallowed Taren.

He reached for the outer wall of the stasis chamber he'd emerged from, trying to ground himself, praying he hadn't fallen into some pit of emptiness.

His hand found the solid wall. He caught his breath.

"Lake?" he called into the darkness, not caring who else might hear him.

Had she returned from the sim? She'd stepped through that impossible doorway. It didn't make sense, but he could picture it in his mind, even jumbled as his thoughts were.

Was she here now, hiding from him in the darkness?

"Lake? Are you there?"

He imagined her crouching between stasis chambers, listening to his hitched breathing, ignoring his calls. Afraid, angry.

"I'm sorry." He pressed the heels of his hands against his eyelids. "For what I did." Opened his eyes again, but he might as well have kept them closed. What had happened to the lights?

Maybe the ship was in its last throes. Maybe it wasn't going to break apart like a cracked egg. It was going to slide into darkness and silence until there was no dividing line between life and death.

He clutched his arms around himself. "I just wanted to wake the girl." The muscles in his legs seized, and he had to lean against the wall of the chamber. "If you're there, please say something. Please?"

He strained for the sound of breathing, for the whisper of bare feet over the steel floor.

The machines hummed. At least they were still working.

He turned back the way he had come and groped for the door of the stasis chamber. Maybe Lake hadn't left the sim after all.

His throat ached, and he remembered now that he'd left water outside the door of his chamber before he'd gone in. He knelt, felt for the cup. But he couldn't find it, and the failure was too much to bear.

He abandoned the task, brittle with despair. *The lights are out, and I'm all alone.*

He forced himself back into the stasis chamber. He'd go back into the sim and find Lake.

Would she understand why he'd done what he'd done?

Without her, you're all alone.

Would she understand that they had to wake the sleepers?

They had so little time left.

20

LAKE

Lake climbed down the promontory, gripping tree roots and then rocks, trying not to think any more about what Taren had done. Lowering herself into the belly of the sim while her heart sank, sank.

At her back, the distant globe of light sent slanting rays that never shifted. The globe was stuck in place, a frozen sun.

I've been here before. I remember this place.

How can that be?

Above her, Willow clambered over rocky ledges, faster and faster until Lake had to warn her, "Go slow, Will."

"What does it matter? Figments can't get hurt."

Lake's heart took another tumble. "I don't want to see you fall."

They passed into deep blue light, sunlight filtered through the strange canopy. It caught the droplets in the air from the waterfall and made them glow. Lake dropped to the dirt and almost expected the thick air to slow her descent. It smelled of cedar and cinnamon and the mineral tang of wet rock.

Willow followed her through the trees, the chilly mist. They found the river, a silvery ribbon. On the opposite bank, a rocky slope drank sunlight so that to look across the river was to peer into near-darkness.

This is what it would be like if you could walk the world faster than the sun rose. Day to twilight to night.

"Now what?" Willow said. All wonder lost on her, apparently.

Lake turned to find her scaling a boulder at the edge of the water, and then realized it wasn't a boulder but a webbed shell long ago discarded by some huge animal. Another mark of this place's oddness.

Lake peered past, into the trees, considering Willow's question. *This place is full of secrets.*

Willow shivered in the cool mist floating from the waterfall. "Do you think Ransom got out of the Battery?"

Lake's stomach twisted. *He should never have gone there.* "I hope so."

Willow looked at her for a long moment. "You weren't trying to wake Eden. I could tell."

The air no longer felt cool and thick and magical. It collected on Lake's bare arms like chilly glass scales. "I wanted to give Ransom a chance to get away. I messed everything up."

"Do you think Ransom got out of the Battery?" Willow asked again.

"You're repeating yourself." Lake rubbed her hands over her damp arms, shivering.

"He showed up in the Battery. He shows up when you want him to, doesn't he?"

Something chittered in the trees—birds or bugs, the sound pitched high so that Willow's question seemed to go on and on.

"There's something strange about him," Lake said. "He can't leave the sim, he never tells me about his past."

"He shows up—"

Lake cut in before Willow could repeat herself again. "Do you think . . ." She swallowed cold, wet air. "Is he like you?"

"Like me?"

"He only shows up where I go."

Willow gazed at the river. Its silver glow made her eyes flash. "Like me."

A figment.

Lake crouched on the gravel bank. She felt like crumpling. The cold rocks bit into her fingertips as she put a hand down on either side to steady herself. "I don't think he knows."

"Where did he come from?"

"He was just . . . *there,* on the beach, one of the first places I remember in the sim."

"But where did he *come* from?"

Lake shook her head. "I don't know. Maybe he was a boy I saw once in real life and don't remember. Maybe the sim does that—makes people appear from the deepest corners of your mind."

"Taren told me he had a dog in the sim that he didn't have in real life."

"Ransom's not a stray."

Willow wandered over and put her hand on Lake's shoulder. "And even so, he follows you. *Everyone* follows you."

Lake peered up at her, wondering what she meant.

"People, figments. You open doors, and they walk through."

"It's never that easy," Lake said.

"They want the truth, and you give it to them," Willow said. "You give it to them like it's a gift and not a weapon."

"*Is* it a gift? A dying ship?"

"They won't be on a ship forever."

"I hope not." Lake let out a shuddering breath. "But what about when we all go home? What's waiting for us there, Will? I don't know if it'll be any better than what we have on the ship."

She pressed her cheek against Willow's hand on her shoulder. *And* you *won't be there.*

The cold rocks at her fingertips felt oddly smooth, and not as cold as before. She looked down—and saw a plastic pipe under her right hand. One end was submerged in the water, weighted with piled rocks.

She stood, tracing its length with her gaze. The other end of it disappeared into the trees.

"What is it?" Willow asked.

"A pipe. For delivering water. To someone's camp, I think."

They followed it into the forest, where it cut past trees and almost disappeared under fallen skeins of soft bark.

"There!" Willow gasped, pointing.

Under the trees sat a dome-shaped shelter. A frame of crisscrossing metal struts showed through a covering of stretched bark. A fine layer of dirt and bits of dried membrane-leaves sheathed all, evidence that the shelter had been here some time.

Beyond, tucked behind trees: more shelters. A dozen, at least, all darkened with dirt and debris.

Lake wandered among them, listening for signs of life, hearing only the rustle of the canopy overhead, the trickle of water through the pipe at her feet. Willow darted ahead and then stopped at the opening of a shelter, where a flap of bark hung loose.

Lake followed, her steps heavier, reluctant. *Is someone inside?*

Willow pulled back the flap and peered inside. A question showed on her face. She turned and gave Lake an uncertain look. Then she ducked into the shelter.

"Will." Lake hurried after her. She slipped into the shelter.

Inside: two camp beds, a low plastic table, a floor of brushed dirt. A jug half-filled with water. A pile of fruit pits.

"Look at this." Willow lifted a pair of goggles from an open case and pulled them over her head. She fumbled with a switch at the side of one lens. "Oooooh. There are little marks painted on the tent."

"Let me see."

Willow handed over the goggles, and Lake pulled them on. On the underside of the bark-tent, tiny glowing specks appeared, painted constellations.

"Someone painted stars," Lake said, pulling off the goggles. "With infrared paint, I think."

She found that Willow was staring up at her, brow furrowed in consternation. "Lake."

"What?"

Willow pointed.

The low light cast a dreamlike spell. Lake felt as if she were watching herself move toward the bed. She lifted the bark-felt blanket to read the name stitched unevenly into the material.

Her own name.

Willow crouched near the other bed. Next to her, the corner of the blanket showed another name: *WILLOW*.

Lake dropped onto the first bed—her bed? All her breath gone. Her thoughts churned faster than the water at the falls.

"Did we live here?" Willow asked. "A long time ago?"

Lake tried to sort through her tangled thoughts. "Did we live in a lost world hidden in the sim?"

Is that why I dream about this place?

"I think I only go where you take me in the sim," Willow said. "But I'm not sure. I have a hard time remembering."

"I have a hard time too." Lake thought of something Taren had once said. "It's like when you have different dreams one after another. You might remember the last dream, but not the earlier ones—not really."

"You think we lived here, but we forgot?"

Lake touched the felt blanket. Looked at the low table where she and Willow had feasted on tree fruit. Touched the bark-wall she had woken next to every morning.

I do remember. "Yes, I think we lived here. You and I. I think this was home when I first arrived in the sim."

A home for a sleeper and a figment.

Her memories of it came needling to the surface of her mind. The weight of the blanket over her at night, Willow's sleeping face in the twilight glow. "Someone made this place for us to live."

How many shelters sat under the trees? A dozen? More? How many people had lived here?

Lake moved to the doorway, pushed the flap aside. *What does it matter?* But she was tearing through the camp now, pushing farther into the trees, taking in the sight of shelter after shelter—

Dozens of them. Enough for a hundred and fifty people.

We all *lived here.*

Someone made this place to be a home for every sleeper on the ship.

But who would do that? It was the most dangerous thing possible, making a home that sleepers would never want to leave. Worse than bunkers, worse than childhood bedrooms or warm kitchens. A beautiful dream that no one would trade for reality.

And yet . . .

We did *leave. We pushed into other pockets of the sim. How?*

Willow brushed up next to her, leaned her weight against Lake's arm. "I found something in one of the shelters." She held out her palm, where a silver badge gleamed: a pair of wings sprouting from a star.

Lake took it with trembling fingers. "Captain's wings."

"He didn't die in stasis."

"No, it doesn't look like he did." Lake studied the badge as if it might reveal something, help her make sense of the thoughts churning in her mind. "He was here, with the rest of us. Living in these shelters at the heart of his own sim."

She lifted her gaze to the shelters, and then to the billowing canopy overhead. Such a strange and lovely place. The most complex pocket she'd ever seen in the sim.

An intricate world created by a talented architect.

The most talented the sim had ever seen.

White water churned in Lake's head, in her stomach. She closed her fingers so tight over the badge that the wingtips bit into her flesh. "He made this place. The captain."

Who else could have invented such a complex pocket in the sim but the creator of the sim himself?

"Pied piper," Willow said. "Leading everyone into the depths of the sim."

"He must have known we'd have a hard time leaving a place like this—but he made it anyway."

"Why would he do that?"

Lake wanted to go back to the dreamy shelter, crawl into the bed, forget everything else. She wanted to stay here with Willow and pretend no other place existed. But she knew what she needed to do.

The breeze shifted the canopy, and Lake caught sight of the promontory she and Willow had climbed down from. She forced herself to start in that direction.

"Where are we going now?" Willow asked, following.

"To find the captain. He didn't die in stasis like I thought. He was here in these shelters, and now he's somewhere else in the sim."

"You know where." Willow's voice dipped. "Don't you?"

The canopy cast its blue light on Lake's skin, and she had

to remind herself that she wasn't underwater, that she could breathe.

"You can't go there, Lake. You swore you never would."

Lake kept up her determined stride. "It's the only place left in the sim that I've never been to. Which means it's the only place he could be."

"The door you've never been through—the door in the middle of the desert," Willow said. "You know where it leads."

The roar of the distant waterfall echoed through the trees like a warning.

"To a simulated version of the ship," Lake said.

"If you go there, you won't be able to get out. You won't be able to tell that you're not awake on the real ship."

Lake's stride broke. She leaned against the soft bark of a tree, catching her breath. "I have to go. I have to find out—"

"What?" Willow put her back against the tree so that Lake was looking into her blue-tinted face, the face of a ghost.

"Why he made this place for us," Lake said.

"A nice place to wake? A home?"

"A trap. A very pretty grave."

Willow looked back toward the shelters. "But no one is here."

"He didn't dig deep enough."

Overhead, invisible birds called from the branches, their low whistles a long-forgotten music.

"I need to know, Will." Lake dug her fingers into the soft outer layer of bark. "I need to know if the reason he made this place is because it wouldn't matter if we never left it. We've been sleeping for decades, waiting to go back to the surface. Waiting to go home. I need to know why he believes we never can."

Fear darkened Willow's eyes. "If you go there, you might never come back out."

Lake pushed away from the tree. "Then I'd better say my goodbyes."

21

RANSOM

The toothpick bridge lay in ruins on the bar, a jagged mess no less terrible than when it had stood upright. Half-broken or half-built, depending on what Ransom might do with it next. At the moment, he could think of it only as a fence between him and the stranger who had just burst through the door of the pub.

"Is Lake here?" the stranger asked, his gaze roving the room.

Ransom's heart jerked sideways at the mention of Lake's name. "Who's asking?" He moved toward the bat he kept propped against the empty ice bin.

The stranger's gaze snagged on Ransom, focused, unfocused. Something was wrong with this guy. "Taren," he said. "I was with her in the Battery."

Ransom kept the bat low, out of sight. "You were there?"

Confusion lined Taren's brow. He rubbed his hand over his eyes. "Oh. I looked different. But that was me. I'm her friend."

His voice went up a little so it was almost a question. "Do you know where she is? Have you seen her?"

Ransom let go of the bat. His palm had gone sweaty anyway. "Shouldn't *you* know where she is? What happened in the Battery?"

Taren came and braced himself against the bar, as if he were about to be sick. "We . . . got split up. I saw her go through a door."

"I didn't see any doors down there. Just empty doorways, thanks to Eden's paranoia."

"I think Lake made one. With the tar."

It was Ransom's turn to grip the bar. "But Lake got out?"

Taren nodded. He sank onto a stool and hunched over the bar as if giving in at last to long-felt exhaustion.

"And now you can't find her." Ransom touched an empty glass under the bar and wished there were something in it, even just water to cool the heat blossoming through his head.

"We had a plan going in," Taren mumbled to the bar. "But it didn't work. We were trapped."

Ransom was having a hard time following. And the hollow tone of Taren's voice had him nervous.

"Everything went wrong," Taren said. "Eden's soldiers started coming at me. So I fought back."

"And Lake left without you?" Something wasn't adding up.

Taren lifted his head. He glanced at Ransom like he was surprised to see him there, like he'd only been talking to himself.

Maybe he is. Maybe I'm not here at all and I'm only kidding myself. The amount of time he'd spent in the sim—his whole life, it seemed. It was more real to him than reality.

"She escaped," Taren said. "I fought. With the tar."

Some long-dormant creature awoke in Ransom's chest. It slithered around his heart, wrapped around his rib cage.

Taren sat frozen, his eyes heavy with despair. "Do you know anything about tar? What it does?"

Ransom's stomach roiled. Yes, he knew.

Someone had followed him here once. When? He couldn't remember. Time felt slippery to him. Ransom had had to fight the guy off with a bat, even as the guy came at him with the tar squirming in a lead cup.

He looked to the end of the bar now, where tar still glinted deep within the wood, boring its way downward like a worm. He thought he could hear it chewing.

He'd seen tar once before, too. He'd seen what it could do to people.

The creature in his chest slithered down into his stomach and coiled there, cold and heavy.

"You shouldn't use it," he told Taren. "It's the worst thing you can do."

Taren's hands shook on the bar. "They might be okay. They might have survived. I didn't mean to hurt them, I just wanted to get out. Do you think they might . . . ? Do you think they're okay?" He looked at Ransom, his gaze pleading.

But Ransom had seen tar, and what it did to people. What it did to those who touched it, and what it did to those who used it. "Sometimes it wakes them. Sometimes it sends them into shock and they don't survive."

"How often? Do you know? If I used it on five people . . ." His throat moved as he swallowed. "Ten . . ."

Ransom tried to tamp down his disgust. "You can't do that again. Don't ever use it." Images flashed in his mind, and he tried to push them away. "You think it'll save you, but tar destroys. And if you use it enough, you become the destroyer."

Taren shook. His chest heaved. Misery rolled off his skin and choked the air like smoke. "Do you know how I got on this ship? How we all did? Not by luck—that's what everyone says, but it's not true. I might have been given a spot on board, but I *chose* to accept it. I knew by taking a spot I was dooming everyone who didn't get one. But I went along with it anyway. Because I didn't want to die. I wanted to live." His gaze went heavy with dread. "It's the selfish who survive."

Ransom looked at the coin on the bar top, the one he'd made, with the billowing tree. "No. Not even them."

He'd tried so hard to lock the memories away. He thought he'd left them behind in that lost world at the heart of the sim. "I used the tar once," he said, "to defend myself."

Taren went still, tense.

"But it didn't save me." Ransom's mouth filled with the metallic tang of regret. "I'm still here in the sim, marked for death like everyone else."

"I've never seen you on the ship before," Taren said slowly, as if the realization were only just coming to him. "Didn't Lake say you were a sleeper?"

"I used to think it was only a matter of time until all the sleepers in the sim woke. But they never will. As long as one person is stuck in the sim, everyone else is doomed."

"I can help you wake."

Ransom gave him a rueful smile. "Lake tried."

"There's more than one way to wake a sleeper."

The lights flickered, responding to Ransom's unsteady nerves.

"You ever wonder why you spend your time in an empty pub?" Taren asked him. "Why there's nothing here to drink, no people or music—"

Ransom flicked his head and a piano started playing in a back room that didn't exist. He knew what Taren was trying to do: use confusion to wake him.

But Ransom was no ordinary sleeper. Unlike other sleepers, he knew he was in a simulation.

Taren hesitated, thrown off by the music. "You never eat, never sleep. Never see any change in this place from day to night."

Ransom offered him a steely smile. "That game doesn't work on me. You can't wake me to a reality I already know about."

"You walk through doors," Taren said, his voice faltering, "and they lead somewhere they shouldn't."

"I wait and wait," Ransom said, taking over for him, "for the sim to dissolve, the ship to die—and me to go with it."

Taren swayed on his stool, lapsing into confusion. "You know about the ship? You know you're in a sim—but you don't wake. It doesn't make any sense."

At the end of the bar, the tar bubbled up from its wormhole.

Taren stood, transfixed by the sight of it, and edged down the length of the bar to the tiny wormhole. "I've never seen you on the ship," he said to Ransom, "but you know you're in a sim. Do you ever leave? Are you real?"

The tar bubbled higher out of the wood, responding to Taren's confusion.

Taren's gaze went unfocused. "I've walked through doors that lead to places they shouldn't lead. Walked out strange exits, onto a dying ship. I've seen things that shouldn't exist. My own brother—" He broke off.

But it was enough. His confusion sent the tar bubbling over. A stream of it trickled down the bar, carving a line in the wood, snaking under the broken toothpick-bridge to where Ransom stood.

Ransom scrambled back. He'd never seen someone do that before—use their own confusion to create tar. His gaze snapped to Taren, who seemed to have shaken off his confusion. He was looking down at his own forearm, and where tattooed stars formed a scattered constellation.

"Why did you do that?" Ransom asked, eyeing the trickling tar again. "Are you going to use it on me now?" He wanted to reach for his bat, but that would bring him closer to the tar still snaking its way down the bar top.

"No," Taren said, a note of defensiveness in his voice. "You said no one could wake you. You said you'd die if you stayed trapped in the sim."

The tar etched a groove into the wood, a deep scar that would never come out.

"I was going to give you a chance to use it on yourself," Taren explained.

Ransom's stomach dropped.

"I don't know if you'll survive it," Taren admitted. "Is it better than being trapped here and going down with the ship?"

Ransom knew what tar could do to a person. He'd seen it.

He hadn't known, until the moment he used it in self-defense, that he was capable of wielding such a weapon. Did that absolve him? Did his regret?

The tar destroys, and I'm a destroyer.

He wasn't sure what *else* he was, but he knew he was *that*.

Whenever Lake tried to ask him about his past, he could feel the memory of that act snaking around his heart. When she tried to save him from the sim, the truth hissed in his ear: he was too tainted to live in a world outside the sim.

He had destroyed, and he would surely bring destruction with him.

The tar wormed closer to the edge of the wood, and Ransom realized that he had stepped toward it, had lifted his hand . . .

He jerked back. The glasses on the shelf behind him rattled and dropped to the floor.

In the same moment, the door to the pub opened wider, and Lake stood staring in horror at the scene before her. She looked to Ransom, to the tar, to Taren backing away from the crash of breaking glass.

"Lake, it's okay," Ransom said.

Taren stood near the bar, mouth open, not saying anything. "You don't have to use it on Ransom," Lake told him.

"No," Taren said, "I wasn't—"

"He's not a sleeper," she cut in.

The glass at Ransom's feet popped and crunched as he stepped toward the bar, trying to pull Lake's gaze. "Lake." The sight of the tar forced him back again, and the betrayed look in Lake's eyes.

"He never wakes," Lake went on. "Never leaves the sim. Shows up in places where I go. Knows my thoughts, sees my dreams." Her gaze fell on the coin still sitting on the bar.

"It's not true," Ransom said, his throat full of broken glass.

Lake shook her head, a pained look in her eyes. "Even Willow doesn't try to tell me that."

Taren looked from Lake to Ransom, a deep line between his brows. "He's a figment?"

Stuck in the sim so long it feels like a lifetime. But Lake was wrong. Wasn't she? Ransom's legs went weak and he had to clutch the shelf behind him to stay standing.

"The most complex figment I've ever encountered," Lake said. "But that's probably my own fault. I spent all my time with him when I first arrived in the sim."

Ransom tried again: "Lake—"

"I came to say goodbye," she cut in.

"What?" A cold hand clutched Ransom's heart. "Where are you going?"

Something silver glinted between her fingers. "The captain is alive," she said, opening her hand to reveal a winged badge. "I'm going to find him."

"Let me come with you," Taren said, stepping toward her.

But Lake drew back. "I'm going alone. I found something at the center of the sim. Something I need answers for."

"What did you find?" Taren asked.

Ransom already knew. He'd seen it himself, long ago. "You found it?" he asked Lake. "Your world of blue trees?"

"And a sun that never sets." Lake studied him, deep in thought.

"What are you talking about?" Taren asked. "What is this place?"

Lake didn't seem to have heard him. She backed toward the door, her face still lined in thought. "The captain knows."

Ransom wanted to stop her. He wanted to explain why he'd never told her about the lost world at the heart of the sim and what had happened there and why he'd been too ashamed to explain before.

But he saw the way she kept her distance from Taren, now that she'd seen him use the tar.

"Will I see you again?" Ransom asked Lake.

She looked down at the metal wings in her hand. "No." Then she turned and vanished through the door.

22

LAKE

As Lake stepped out of the pub, a hand locked around her forearm.

She tried to pull free—but too late. In a moment, she had left the pub for a new pocket of the sim, and she wasn't alone. Taren stood next to her, still gripping her arm.

She wrenched free. "What're you—"

"Wait, Lake." He held his palms out. "I just want to talk."

Behind him: a desert landscape. Heat rippled over red-brown dirt. Low mountains slumped at the horizon.

Lake edged back from Taren. "What you did in the Battery . . ."

Dark circles showed under Taren's eyes. He lifted an unsteady hand to clutch the side of his head. "I don't feel right. I'm in a nightmare, and there's nothing to wake to."

The despair in his voice pulled at her. "You shouldn't be in the sim. Go back to the ship."

"The ship—another nightmare."

She couldn't dispute it. "You can't come with me."

"Why not? Where are we?"

Lake turned. Found proof that sometimes the sim gave you things that were only as strange as real life: Row after row of gleaming jet planes stretched to the horizon. Red-and-blue-striped fuselages, dolphin-nosed cockpits, dirt-streaked bellies. They all stood lined up in the desert, mechanical wonders never to be used again. "We're in an airplane boneyard in the Mojave Desert," she told Taren.

"The door in the middle of the desert," Taren said, his voice lowering to a rasp. "You told me about this once."

A small voice behind Lake said, "Don't let her go in there, Taren." Lake turned back to find Willow standing next to Taren, squinting into the bright distance. "It's a graveyard. She'll never come out."

"No, Will." Lake stepped close to her and pushed her messy hair behind her ears. "A *boneyard*. It's just a place where people come out and scavenge for parts for other planes."

"Why are we here?" Taren asked.

"The captain of the ship has a pilot's license," Lake said. "You don't start out flying a spaceship without practicing on something smaller first."

"She's going to talk to him," Willow said.

"What, you think he's just been sitting in a cockpit this whole time, pretending to steer a dead airplane?" Taren said.

"No, he's not on an airplane." Lake lifted a hand to shield her eyes from the glare. In the distance, she spotted what she'd come here for: a Boeing 747 with a curious cabin door.

Taren followed her gaze. "What's in there?" Panicked edge to his voice. "Willow, what's through that door?"

Willow eyed him warily, edged closer to Lake. She hadn't forgotten about the Battery either, it seemed. "A simulated version of the ship, best guess. It looks just like the doors on the ship, right, Lake?"

"The captain's through there," Lake said. "He has to be."

Taren caught Lake's arm again. "You want to go into a pocket of the sim that looks just like the ship?"

She speared him with a look that made him let go. "I didn't ask you to come with me," she said.

"She'll never come out," Willow said again, and Lake's ribs tightened around her lungs.

"Willow's right," Taren said. "How are you going to remember you're not really on the ship?"

Lake's breath kept coming short. "You know another way I can talk to the captain?"

"And what's he going to tell you? You think he knows a better way to wake the sleepers?"

"No. I don't think he's interested in waking the sleepers at all. But if he knows how we got into this mess, maybe he knows if there's any way out."

"There *is* a way out. Wake the sleepers. Get off the ship."

"You haven't seen what I've seen. You don't understand what's at the heart of the sim."

"Don't do this. It'll only make everything worse—one more sleeper trapped in the sim."

Lake glared at him. The heat of the desert air was no match for the heat of the anger and shock that had been bubbling inside her since the Battery. "Are you going to lock me up, like they do on the ship?" *Or worse*—"Are you going to find some tar?"

Taren shrank back, wounded.

Lake felt a pang of guilt. But it quickly vanished as she turned toward the boneyard, the rows of sand-blown airplanes. "Come on, Willow. If you're coming."

They left Taren.

A gust of warm wind sprayed dirt over tufted desert weeds and against their shins as they plodded toward the plane in the close heat.

"You know how the Egyptians buried their leaders in the desert?" Willow said. "Or, entombed them, I guess?"

"The captain's not inside the airplane," Lake said. "He's no mummy. This is just where the door to the sim-ship is."

"They killed cats and put them in the tombs with the mummies. Servants, too."

Lake stopped short of the plane. She leaned down so she was eye level with Willow. "The captain isn't a pharaoh. We aren't his cats." She did her best to ignore the gnawing in her stomach as she straightened. "Or his dead servants."

"Not yet," Willow said.

Lake started up the wheeled staircase, her feet heavy as lead. "When we step through that door, you have to stay close. Help me remember it's a simulation."

Sweat trickled down Lake's back. She focused on that, and on the pounding in her head, instead of on the dread creeping over her. She opened the slick black door.

A hallway greeted her, exactly like the hallways on the ship. Flickering lights overhead, metal floor beneath her boots.

Her heart pounded as she crept along the passage. Hum of air vents, roar of her breathing. She looked over her shoulder, past Willow, to the door they'd come through, wondering if she'd remember how to find it again. *I said my goodbyes.*

Not very good ones.

Her heart sank with the weight of what she'd left behind: Taren, alone and confused in the desert, and Ransom . . .

The boy she'd spent her frozen days with—days when time stood still and they didn't want anything more than each other.

The boy she'd invented. A figment.

Her heart sank further, and she forced herself to keep walking. At the end of the hallway: a door. Locked, like so many of the doors on the ship were.

She touched the handle. Pushed.

The door opened. But then, the sim often surprised her.

She held the door for Willow, who passed her with a worried look. "Cats," she said darkly.

Lake swallowed. She let the door close behind them and slipped past Willow to lead her down another hallway. *Is this the way to the captain's controls?* She didn't know what it would look like—if the captain had to fly the ship in a cockpit that looked out at the stars, or if he only sat in a room full of computer screens. She turned the corner, oddly interested to find out.

It wasn't a cockpit, or a computer lab, or anything Lake would have expected. It was several rows of leather airplane seats, like a first-class cabin. A flight attendant pushed a cart up the aisle, her smile firm, her gaze empty. A figment.

The cart stopped three feet from where Lake stood. Rattle of ice. Pop of soda tab. Smell of scotch. A voice from one of the seats said, "Don't forget the straw."

Lake inched forward until the passenger came into view: a man with wispy yellow hair, lightly sweating in a blue suit jacket.

Yeah, she knew him.

Had seen him on TV, and lingering with the principal in the halls of her school, eyeing students like you'd inspect eggs in a carton at the grocery store.

Captain of the ship. Pied piper.

Master of the broken vessel that was taking them all down with it.

She drew in a breath so hot with anger it might sear her lungs, and took another step forward.

The line between his brows said he'd noticed her. "You the captain of this ship?" she asked him.

The line deepened. Did he remember, or did he think he was on an airplane?

The flight attendant held out his drink. He didn't take it from her, just sipped from the straw.

Willow leaned around Lake to get a look. "This is him?"

"A real sleeper." Lake couldn't stop watching the captain sip the drink the woman held, as distasteful as she found the sight.

"Can we order a drink?" Willow whispered to Lake. "Just root beer or something?"

Lake stepped up to the cart and grabbed a can of root beer, passed it back. "You've been sleeping a long time," she said to the captain. "Don't you think it's time you woke up?"

He pushed his straw away with his lips and leaned his head back against the seat. "You know, I recognize you. Took me a minute. Not as sharp as I used to be."

Lake's stomach twisted. She should probably be happy he wasn't totally deluded, but it only made her feel like an egg in a carton. "You took us from our parents."

His eyes widened. "Yes, I saved you."

"Like a person saves dessert for the end."

The captain frowned at her. The flight attendant stood smiling next to him, her hand still holding out the drink. Such a disorienting picture.

"You decided the situation was hopeless, so you came out here to hide from it all?" Lake asked.

The line appeared between his brows again, but this time a shadow passed over his expression. "Hide . . ." he said quietly.

Unnerving.

The captain jerked his head, signaling to the attendant to take his drink away. "You see the situation I'm in," he said to Lake.

Lake pushed the cart and took a reluctant step forward so that the captain came into full view.

His back was pressed deep into the seat, and his arms in their blue suit sleeves—

They were melded to the armrests. Sunk so deep in leather and plastic, it almost wasn't accurate to say he *had* arms any-more.

She swallowed her revulsion. "What's happening to you?"

"I made sure the ship knew that when everyone else woke up, I should go to sleep forever." The captain nodded at the attendant and she pressed a wet towel against his sweaty forehead. "My plan has always been for you children to make your way safely off the ship—and for me to make my exit from the world. I'm not fit for starting over."

Safely off the ship. Lake swallowed the bitterness creeping up the back of her throat.

"You're dying?" Willow asked the captain.

"Yes," the captain replied with a rueful smile. "I've used Paracosm to leave reality so many times. But this will be the last. Death will be the strangest exit yet."

Lake couldn't find it in her heart to feel sorry for him. "If you wanted us to get safely off the ship, why'd you program it not to let us off until everyone leaves the sim?"

The captain frowned. "I didn't. But I've long suspected that the ever-growing simulation was straining the ship, keeping it from following protools."

"Then it amounts to the same thing—we can't control the ship until all the sleepers wake and their pockets of the sim close. Why didn't the ship try to wake us sooner?"

"The ship sends out probes once a year," the captain explained. "The probes collect data about the surface conditions, so it knows when to wake us."

"Yes, I've seen the data. Craters and fire and smoke and—"

"No, those are the pockets of the sim the passengers created themselves. Out of fear for what they would find when they went home to the surface."

"Then what's Earth's surface really like now?"

The captain's cheek twitched, and Lake half waited for the attendant to scratch it for him. "The probes went out. Year after year, decade after decade. But the improvement we hoped for . . . never came."

Lake gripped the back of a seat, hit hard by a wave of disappointment. She'd known, hadn't she? As soon as she'd realized that the captain had created that lovely home with the shelters under the trees—she'd understood that he believed they'd never get home. "Then the ship woke us only to die. And you made the world at the heart of the sim to ease our passing."

The captain squirmed in his seat. His eyes went unfocused. "There's a creature at the heart of the simulation. That's why we had to leave that place." He mumbled something more, words Lake couldn't make out.

She leaned closer, listening. But she couldn't make sense of his mutterings. "A creature?" she tried. "In the sim?"

His head sank back so deeply into the seat, Lake wondered if it would lodge there forever. "I didn't create it."

"You didn't create the creature? Then where did it come from?"

He no longer seemed aware that anyone else was with him, just went on whispering to himself about things Lake could not make sense of.

"*Hey,*" she growled. "You can't just check out. Your ship is falling to pieces. We're not going to get *safely off*. We're going to die unless you can find some way to fix it."

The captain blinked up at her.

"You took us from our families. Said you were going to save us." Lake gripped the seat back. "You told us we could find a way to start over once we woke from stasis."

"Start over. Yes, but you see what we've done to our home. What's to keep us from making the same mistakes again? We're set in our ways—but that's why I brought only young people. It's our only chance for doing anything differently."

Were they doing anything differently? Retreating to odd fortresses, stockpiling weapons.

But that hardly mattered now. "Your ship is broken. We *can't* go home. Even if there were anything left for us on the surface, we can't get there."

The captain started mumbling again, and twitching in his seat, as if overwhelmed by the venom of her accusations.

"Why did you even bring us on this ship? You brought us here to die."

Behind her, Willow touched her arm. Lake cringed with guilt at the thought that her words had frightened Willow. But then a small, cold hand slipped into Lake's and squeezed, and Lake realized her sister was trying to comfort her.

The captain gave up his mumblings and cast his gaze toward the round window that looked out at nothing. "When I first had this ship built, it was meant for exploration," he said. "It would take us to places as untouched as Earth had once been. A long time ago, the future used to be something to build toward. Technology was a vehicle to bring us into golden days. Now it's just a game of who's clever enough to escape."

"Of who can manage to own a ship, you mean," Lake said. "Or a bunker, or a cache of supplies."

"You think my wealth makes me evil. But it's wealth that built this marvel." He looked around the dusty cabin, as though old airplane seats were worth getting excited over.

"Your marvel is broken," Lake told him. "Most of it's locked down, we can't access even half of it. We can't get to any kind of controls to fix anything."

"But here in the sim . . ." He seemed to forget that he was speaking and only stared ahead at the seat in front of him.

"The sim is different. There might be controls here, but—"

"Yes." The captain squinted in thought. "And since the simulation is connected to the program that runs the ship, those controls might just fix the real ship . . ." He trailed off again, but Lake had heard enough to make her itch with hot, dangerous hope.

It was a strange idea, using the sim to affect reality. But she could try it.

But the sleepers will still be trapped in the sim. And the sim will go on straining the ship's systems until we get them out.

"Lake?" Willow said behind her. "Are we going to search for the controls?"

Lake was still lost in thought. "Is there a way . . ." Her heart thudded in her chest. "Do you know a way to wake all the sleepers at once?" she asked the captain.

She shrank from the dread her own words awakened in her. *There* is *a way—with the tar.*

But could there be another way?

"A way that won't send the sleepers into shock?" she added.

"Pull the plug on the whole program?" He closed his eyes, and his skin suddenly looked waxy in the low light. "They're embedded too deeply for that now."

Lake swallowed disappointment. "Let's go, Will."

The flight attendant beckoned to them and then pointed to a door at the far end of the room.

"The ship's controls are there?" Lake asked, unsettled by the woman's empty smile.

She answered only by pulling the cart back and then disappearing through the door.

Lake glanced back at Willow, unsure. Willow only shrugged and gulped down the last of her soda. She left the empty can on a seat, and then the two of them approached the door.

23

TAREN

Taren left the desert for a more familiar pocket of the sim: the neighborhood where Lake had taken him on his first trip back into the sim.

The one so close to his own neighborhood.

"Never go into your own house." But he had to. He felt as if he were becoming a figment of himself, a hollow ghost of who he had been before all of this had started.

When he'd walked through that door in the tiger yard and left the sim, had he left himself, too?

The houses along the street looked oddly one-dimensional, as if painted onto a backdrop. Taren stared at the closest one and realized it was nothing more than a blurry block of color behind a ragged fence of weeds. A hole stood where the door should be, a gaping mouth.

The street narrowed sharply, and then Taren came to the end of it, a wall painted to give the illusion that the road continued on. He pushed on the wall. It gave.

"Make this street lead to my house," he commanded.

The wall expanded, then melted under his touch, opening the road so that Taren could step through.

And here was his house. Blistered paint, sagging roof, bowed walls—a house ruined by decades of neglect. *This is what it looks like down on Earth.* His heart sank.

He stepped onto the tilted porch. Stood for a long moment like a patient visitor. He knew what he needed to do before he went inside.

He breathed weed-scented air.

Finally turned his forearm stars-up.

He touched one of the inked stars and then dragged his finger to his wrist, taking the star with it. In a moment, he'd rearranged the entire constellation, as simple as a surgeon re-arranging his own veins.

Now he wouldn't get trapped in his own sim-home. Much as a part of him wanted to.

He opened the door.

His dog trotted to meet him the moment he stepped inside. Taren dropped to his knees and scratched the dog's boxy head, clutched his warm, furry body. "You been eating? Let's get you some water."

The dog wasn't real, didn't need water. But it felt good to snatch a bowl from the cabinet, fill it with rainwater from the barrel out front, set it before the wriggling dog. Taren leaned against the wall while the dog drank, imagining the house as it had once been. The sound of his mother dropping her keys on the counter, of his dad digging through rustling bags of groceries. He wandered down the hall to the door of his own bedroom. If he stepped inside, would he see himself hunched over his desk?

He hurried on, to the kitchen. He touched the calendar on the wall, and the drawing tacked next to it of a tall-peaked house and cloud-shaped trees. Sat at the table, smelling his dad's coffee, his mom's pancakes. Kept checking his tattoo so he'd remember not to stay too long.

The whole time, the back door trembled against a buffering wind. Shut tight against Taren's anxious thoughts: his parents probably hadn't survived nuclear winter. Or they might have, but enough years might have passed to claim their lives anyway. Taren couldn't stand thinking of them waiting for a son who hadn't returned. But if they weren't waiting for him, did he still want to go home to the surface?

He stood from the table, his eyes on the trembling door. He knew what lay out there. He'd seen it last time he'd come to his sim-house. He forced himself to go to the door, open it.

A massive crater comprised the entire landscape, the size of ten neighborhoods together. Gusting wind whipped up thin plumes of dirt like smoke. The churned earth seemed ready to become a grave.

It's not real. This is just a simulation.

The crater exhaled smoke. A noise rose from its depths, a rumble of fractured earth. A voice. *Do you want to survive?* it asked Taren.

Taren quaked. He had boarded a ship, slept for decades, escaped the sim, fought his way back through it. "Yes," he answered.

The sides of the crater shifted, crumbled. The sound of

trickling dirt was the sticky sound of a throat opening. *Do you know what you need to do?*

Taren went on quaking.

He had to wake the sleepers. There was no getting out of it. Wake them or die.

His arm throbbed, and he looked down to see his distorted tattoo, the stars all wrong. He remembered what Ransom had told him: *You use the tar, you become the destroyer.* He could feel it already—he was losing himself. The tar had somehow gotten inside him and was eating up everything that made him who he was.

Was there another way?

He pictured Lake in the desert. *"You haven't seen what I've seen. You don't understand what's at the heart of the sim."*

He backed away from the door, the crater.

If he carved a door in the wall, the way Lake had in the cavern—what would he find beyond it, in the heart of the sim?

To make a door, he would need tar.

He took a deep breath, bracing himself for what he had to do: create more tar.

You woke in a simulation, and then you woke to reality, he told himself. *How do you know, each time you wake, that you're waking at all?* He dug his fingers into his scalp, reeling against the confusion that fogged his brain. He pressed into the feeling, searching his mind for the thoughts that most threatened to break his grip on reality—the only way to make the tar he needed.

They've left you to survive on your own. But only tar offers

survival.

And yet, if you use it, there will be no waking, only darkness forever—

He fell to his knees with a groan.

A wave of nausea rolled over him. He clutched his forearm, where his tattoo showed. For a moment, he couldn't understand why the stars were in the wrong place. And then it came to him. *The sim. I'm a prisoner.*

The fog of confusion rolled away.

At his feet, in the join between the wall and the floor, an inky string of tar wormed its way free. Taren scuttled back from it. He picked up a rag from the kitchen counter and carefully dipped it in the wriggling tar.

"Please don't touch it, *please,*" he murmured to himself, trying his best not to imagine the tar seeping through the cloth and infecting his skin.

As quick as he could, he smeared the tar over the wall next to the back door.

The wall crumbled. Taren used the rag to jab at the disintegrating wall, below where the tar had cut to form the top of a doorway. The wall turned to dust and rained onto the tile. Taren dropped the rag.

Through the opening in the wall, he spied only darkness.

Was this the lost world Lake had found? A pitch-black nightscape?

Taren stepped through, uncertain. He smelled salt water and rock, heard the crash of distant waves, felt a chill of icy wind over his skin.

He crept forward. Rocky slope under his feet. He slipped on the uneven ground and fell to his arms and knees.

What is this place?

In the distance: the mournful waves. No—something more, another sound. An eerie cry, like the keening of a creature.

Taren scrambled over the rocks on his hands and feet. *What's out there?*

Up ahead, as though a cold dawn had broken, blue light glowed on a rocky riverbank. Taren shot toward it, away from the creature calling in the darkness.

At the water's edge, the light shone brighter, an early-morning glow. Across the river, a strange forest of billowing trees filtered the low sunlight. And above, on a high promontory, a figure stood surveying the land below.

Eden.

More figures gathered behind her, and then more, emerging from the trees on a high ledge.

Taren inched back into the darkness.

The sleepers had all left the Battery. There was no point now in waking Eden, or in closing the pocket she'd created.

Taren would have to wake the sleepers one by one. *Before* the ship failed. An impossible task.

Unless he used tar.

He sank to the ground, hands pressed over his face.

He'd have to use tar on every single one of them.

24

LAKE

Lake stepped through the door into a space identical to the dimly lit hallways on the ship. A wave of dizziness made her press her hand against the cool wall to brace herself. She turned back to see Willow closing the door behind them. "The door didn't take us out of the sim?" she asked Willow.

"Well." Willow gave her a grim smile. "I'm still here, so . . ."

Lake's stomach clenched. *Still in the sim.*

And she realized now that if she had wakened from the sim, she would be in a stasis chamber right now, her breath fogging a plastic shell shut tight over her.

"Where are the controls?" Willow looked unimpressed with the empty hallway, the flickering lights.

"Must be somewhere nearby." Lake started down the hallway, trailing her fingers over the wall, hoping the touch of metal could keep her grounded.

"Do you think this will work?" Willow asked. "Do you think the controls in the sim can fix the real ship?"

"The captain said the sim is connected to the program that runs the ship." Lake bit her lip. *Is this too much to hope for?*

But what if it works? What if I can fix the CO$_2$ scrubbers, or unlock the doors?

"He said you can't go home to the surface," Willow reminded her.

Lake tried to keep her breathing steady. "I'll think about that later. Right now, we just need to make sure the ship doesn't quit on us."

The hallway forked, and she stopped, troubled by the distant sounds floating from the branch to her right. "Do you hear that?"

Willow tilted her head, listening. She gave Lake a worried look. "I don't think we're alone."

The sounds grew louder: a distant clatter of activity, a whine of laboring machines, a chorus of anxious voices. "It's the eatery," Lake said. "That's all."

Willow frowned. "The . . . ?"

"One of the few places on the ship not locked down or full of stasis beds."

"But we're not really walking around on the ship right now—it's just the sim."

Lake dug her fingers into her palms, trying to keep herself focused. "The sim-ship must have an eatery just like the real ship."

Willow listened to the distant chaos, her eyes going wide as the voices turned to garbled shouting. "Is the real eatery as terrifying as the sim-eatery?"

"Come on." Lake grabbed her hand and pulled her down

the other hallway, spurred by the sudden echo of footsteps from the eatery. *They're only figments—what can they do?* But she knew from experience that figments felt as solid as real people, in the sim. They could grab and hit and—

Adrenaline surged through her and she quickened her pace.

Then—a door. Lake seized the handle. Locked.

"Over here." Willow pulled Lake toward an open doorway lit by an eerie red glow. "The controls."

The room throbbed. Red lights pulsed from the screens that covered the walls, and from the bulbs overhead. Lake felt she had slipped into the bowels of a beast. *Swallowed by the sim.*

"I hear them coming," Willow said, leaning half-into the doorway.

Lake scanned the readings on the screens, understanding nothing except that the ship's systems were failing. *Even here in the sim, the ship's a mess.*

She touched a screen, hoping it would open access to something—the shuttles, the locks, the stasis machines.

The screen went dark at her touch and then a word bloomed there:

PARACOSM

The program that ran the simulation. Lake tapped on it, but nothing happened.

From the hallway, the sound of thudding footsteps grew louder. "*Lake,*" Willow said.

Lake jabbed her finger against another screen.

Another.

This isn't working.

Grunts and shouts from the hallway.

"I can't get it to work!"

A piercing shriek—

Lake's head snapped up. "Willow?" No Willow in the doorway.

Silence from the hallway.

Lake barreled from the room—into an empty hallway. "Willow?" She crept along, ears pricked. Only the hum of the air vents, the pounding of her heart. *The figments from the eatery—they got her.*

But then, where were the figments now?

She reached the fork in the passage. Hesitated only a moment before choosing the one that went to the eatery.

Still quiet. Even when she reached the door at the end. Even when she opened it.

The eatery was twilight-dim, lit only by a few electric flares scattered over the floor like embers. A glowering boy stood before her: Kyle, the boy she'd argued with about opening the door to Taren's makeshift cell.

"You've been going into the sim, haven't you?" Kyle snarled, his face up-lit by the red light of the flare he clutched. "I've seen you sneaking around the ship." His free hand closed on her wrist, tight as a vise.

"Let go," Lake barked.

He held tight, dragging her into the eatery, past huddled forms and overturned tables. "You're the reason the ship is breaking down. The lights have all gone out, the food is gone."

He's just a figment. This isn't real. This isn't—

He jerked open the door to one of the makeshift cells and shoved her inside.

"Stop," Lake said. "I can't stay here. I have to get out." He'd trap her in the sim. He'd lock her in and she'd never get back to the—

Or . . . wait.

She was already on the ship. Right?

The scene before her was so real. The huddled forms, the glowering boy, the darkened view-screens . . .

Is this the sim or isn't it?

She raked her fingers over her head. *Where's Willow?*

Nowhere.

So is this the sim?

Something trickled down the door to her cell, a shadow darker than the other shadows. *What* is *that?*

The sound of metal scraping over metal startled her. Kyle was dragging a table toward the door of her cell, preparing to block her inside.

Don't let him trap you. A spike of fear drove into her heart.

She started to reach for the door handle, but whatever substance had wormed its way down the glass had dripped onto the metal. Just the tiniest drop, hardly worth worrying over. But Lake didn't want to touch it. It spread even as she watched it, coating the handle with a thin veneer of shadow.

Don't touch it. But the table was moving closer. She'd be trapped.

She wrenched the handle, banging the door against the table Kyle was dragging nearer, and slipped through the narrow opening—

Into the blinding glare of the desert boneyard.

I'm still in the sim.

She should have X'd the door and left the sim, but in her panic, she'd only gone from one pocket to another.

Something clung to the skin of her palm. Lake didn't want to look at it. Forced herself to.

A thin layer of tar. Spreading toward her fingers.

Death, coming for her.

Panic seized her. *I have to get out of the sim.* She found a red-brown pebble at her feet and snatched it up. Drew a tiny X over the door. *Good enough.* Opened the door and stepped through—

Cool darkness. The wheezing of machines.

Lake lifted the plastic lid and tumbled out of the stasis bed.

It's okay. I'm okay.

Her legs were weak, mouth dry. She needed a bathroom and water and someone to tell her she wasn't dying.

She'd have to settle for the company of her own desperation. *As usual.*

The warehouse was pitch-dark. Lake stumbled past stasis

chambers, her fingers brushing over walls to guide her to the warehouse's opening.

The hallway was dark too, but up ahead, an electric flare glowed in the doorway to the eatery. She remembered Kyle's glowering face, his painful grip on her wrist. *He's not here, that wasn't real.*

She crept into the eatery, her skin glowing with the blue light from the flare in the doorway. *What a specter I must be to them.* Faces turned toward her—one she recognized.

"Ajay," she said. "You made it through."

He frowned. "Who are you?"

She'd been in disguise when she'd last seen him. But it didn't matter that he didn't recognize her. She was just glad he'd made it out.

"Please," she said. "Do you have any water? Anything to eat?"

He studied her for a moment longer, his expression softening. "A little." He held out a cup.

She collapsed next to him, all of her strength gone. *Lying in a stasis bed for hours and still exhausted.* But that was what happened when you didn't eat or drink, when you lived on a diet of adrenaline and defeat.

She took the cup from Ajay and drank. The water was gone too fast, and she still shook with thirst and exhaustion.

"Are you okay?" he asked. "Just come from the sim?"

Lake glanced around at the passengers huddled at tables and conspiring in corners. No one seemed to be listening to her conversation with Ajay. She nodded.

"I only just got out," Ajay said. "A girl helped me."

From the far end of the eatery: shouts of distress met with raised voices.

"There are still people stuck in the sim," Ajay told Lake. "We can't get off the ship until someone rescues them."

Lake squeezed her eyes shut, fighting against the nausea roiling in her stomach. *Stuck in the sim or on the ship—it doesn't matter which anymore.* The ship was failing. She hadn't been able to fix any of its problems. It didn't even matter that they couldn't get to the shuttles, because there was nowhere to go. Earth's surface was no longer habitable, would probably never be.

"I told everyone here that the rest of the people trapped in the sim are all in a place called the Battery," Ajay said.

It doesn't matter. Let them stay there. Let them sleep, if all they have to wake for is death.

"The people who are stuck in the Battery don't really want to be there," Ajay said. "They're afraid. They don't think there's anything better waiting for them elsewhere."

"What if they're right?"

Ajay peered around at the shifting silhouettes, the flare-lit faces like masks of misery floating in the darkness. "Do you think they'd leave if we promised them a tour of a spaceship?" he joked.

"I've taken the tour myself. It's not what you'd hope for in a spaceship."

Ajay examined her with pity in his eyes. He shifted so he could pull something from his pocket. "Are you hungry? There isn't much, but you seem like you need this."

He pressed something small and round into her hand. Lake hardly registered it. She wanted to tell Ajay that it didn't matter, that they might as well go back into the sim and find their way to the lost world and wait for the ship to fail . . .

But then she looked down at what was in her hand.

Fruit. Fresh fruit.

"Where did you get this?" she asked, voice trembling.

"Someone found it in a strange metal box."

Lake looked around, and now she realized that the forms huddled together weren't passengers who had given in to despair. They were whispering, passing something hand to hand—fruit.

But where did it come from?

She studied the small globe in her hand, its strange pink flesh. In a flash, she remembered the shelter under the trees that she and Willow had lived in. A bowl of fruit pits sat on a table—the table where she had once feasted on ripe fruit like the globe she held now.

The fruit had come from the sim? That couldn't be possible. Something real couldn't come from a simulation. You couldn't create something in a computer program and then expect it to appear in real life.

The captain's voice went through her head: "*I didn't create it.*"

What hadn't he created? The creature that he believed roamed the lost world?

Or the lost world itself?

"*The ship sends out probes. . . . The probes collect data about the surface conditions.*"

The sim was supposed to replicate surface conditions. It was supposed to show them what life on the surface would be like. But it had failed.

Or had it?

"When I first had this ship built, it was meant for exploration. It would take us to places as untouched as Earth had once been."

The captain hadn't created the lost world at the heart of the sim. The ship had created it, using data from the probes. Data about the surface of the planet.

Only, that planet wasn't Earth.

Lake shook all over. Her fingers pressed into the flesh of the fruit she held. A sweet smell wafted to her. "There's something out there," she breathed.

Ajay leaned closer, trying to hear. "What did you say?"

"There's something waiting for us." *A whole planet, a new world.*

We're not going to die on this ship.

The world at the heart of the sim was a reflection of a real place. Its waterfall, its river, its billowing trees.

And they could go there. If the sleepers left the sim.

It hardly seemed possible. It was a dream, another trick.

And yet, here was the proof, right here in her hand.

She lifted the fruit to her mouth, recalling the sweet-tart taste of it, ready to take a bite.

"What happened to your hand?" Ajay said.

Lake froze. Pulled the untasted fruit away from her mouth. Inspected her palm.

The tar was gone, but the skin had turned ash gray.

Lake dropped the fruit. It hit the floor and burst open. The sweet smell turned her stomach. She touched the gray skin on her palm, and flakes of it fell away.

She had escaped the sim, but not the effects of the tar.

25

LAKE

Poison. The tar in the simulation had poisoned her.

She knew the body could react to what shocked the mind. But how far would the poison spread?

An alarm sounded, jarring Lake out of her thoughts. *What now?*

"It's the CO_2 scrubbers," she heard someone say, and then she spotted the red light flashing near the air vent. "I think they've finally given out."

Next to Lake, Ajay had gone still, his eyes closed. "Ajay?" Lake jostled him and he stirred but didn't wake.

The oxygen is getting low.

She got to her feet and made her way out of the eatery. They couldn't fix the ship—only abandon it. And to do that, they'd have to wake the sleepers.

And how will I manage that?

She didn't know. She only knew she had to hurry.

The stasis warehouse still lay in darkness. Lake groped her way to an open chamber and sent herself into the sim.

She woke in the hills outside the Battery. Blue sky, sculpted clouds. A world she'd never see again. Whatever happened, this would be her last trip into the sim, her last view of home. She let herself feel the loss of it for one long, searing moment. The feathery fennel with its licorice smell. The hawks floating on thermal drafts as if suspended in time. The deer-prints like sigils in the dirt.

And what else? What else will you have to abandon?

She knew, but couldn't admit it to herself.

She forced herself onward, to the concrete temple of the Battery.

No guard at the gates. No voices echoing in the shaft as she climbed down the ladder. No clatter of rocks in the stone city, where steps and doorways stood half-formed.

Smell of mud and minerals in the cavern. Black stains where tar still seeped into rock.

The sleepers had abandoned their city.

Because of me, because of the doorway I opened.

And now it would be so much harder to wake them. Impossible, maybe, considering how little time was left.

Had she doomed them?

Angel of Death.

She walked through the doorway she'd made, into shade cast by blue trees.

Willow appeared at her side, walking toward the precipice with her. "Your hand," she said.

Lake inspected it. Then wished she hadn't. A thin layer of tar clung to her palm, as though it had never left her. The sight made her shake. *It's going to spread.* "It's fine," she lied. No need to scare Willow, who was shaking now too.

"You should leave the sim, before it spreads."

"It's not spreading," Lake said, and that seemed to be true for now at least. "I barely touched any of it."

Willow stared at the tar for a moment longer. Then she darted to a tree whose outer layer of bark had all but sloughed off. She tore a strip of soft bark away and came back to wrap Lake's hand with it.

"No, let me do it," Lake said, rigid with worry to see Willow so close to tar.

"You shouldn't have come back."

"I have to wake the sleepers who left the Battery. There's not much time."

"How are you going to wake them?" Willow asked while Lake finished winding the bark around her own palm.

Lake had no answer.

They came to the edge of the precipice. Below, Lake spied movement beneath the billowing treetops, where she knew the camp lay. If she climbed down and told them about the world that waited for them, would that be enough to convince them to leave the sim?

She had once dreamed of this place in the sim, even looked for it while she wandered pocket after pocket. Eden, too, had searched for this lost world, and had finally given in to its pull. Had they both known, deep down, that they belonged in this place? That it was more real than anything else they'd encountered in the sim? A re-creation of a real world that waited for them.

Would that feeling be enough to free Eden and the other sleepers, once Lake told them about the planet that awaited them?

She didn't know. She could only try.

"Lake," Willow said, her voice high with alarm.

Lake turned to find Willow staring down the slope they had once used to climb into the lost world. Except there was no slope—only the jagged edge of the rock shelf, and tar still clinging to it.

"They found where we hid the tar," Willow said.

"And they used it to make sure no one could follow them." *How much did they use? How much is left?* When she walked into the camp, would they have more tar waiting for her?

She inspected the bark-bandage over her palm. It had darkened. The tar was starting to seep through.

"How are we going to get down?" Willow asked.

Lake walked back toward the top of the waterfall and peered over the edge. Tried to guess whether the river was too shallow, the drop too long, the rocks too many.

It was their only way down.

"Remember the water park?" Lake asked Willow. "The tall diving platforms?"

"The ones you refused to jump off of?"

Lake shrugged. "Time to redeem myself."

She jumped.

For a long moment, she imagined herself dropping through the atmosphere, bulleting from the ship, a passenger jumping overboard. *Will we make it? When we leave the ship for the planet, will the shuttles know what to do?*

Then she was swallowed by water and fear and doubt, her lungs hardening while she fought toward the surface.

She gasped for breath and looked around for Willow. Maybe she'd stayed up on the rocks.

But then Lake saw her—

Standing on the bank.

With Taren.

How did he get here?

"Will," Lake called, her voice sharper than she'd meant for it to be. She didn't like seeing Willow standing next to Taren, not when she could still so easily recall the anger and determination on his face as he fought the sleepers in the Battery. She scrambled onto the bank and hurried to her.

"Lake," Taren said, relief in his voice. "I didn't know if you'd make it back."

Willow had shed her jacket somewhere, and now she looked like something that had lost its shell. So small and vulnerable. Lake moved between her and Taren.

Taren drew back, stung. He gave Lake a forced smile. "Here," he said, holding out a small, pink globe like the one she'd recently held on the ship. "Fruit from the trees." He pointed at a tree leaning over the river, its branches heavy with more plump fruit.

The smell of it reminded Lake of the ship's eatery, the

huddled forms. The stain spreading over her palm. She couldn't bring herself to reach for the fruit, and Taren finally looked away from her and let his hand drop.

"I think there might be something hiding in the darkness," he said. "An animal."

Lake followed his gaze to the deep gloom that cloaked the other side of the bank. She shivered, still dripping with cold river water.

"I heard it calling," Taren said. He trembled in the same way he did when they were out of the sim and he was weak from stasis. Lake wondered how long it had been since he'd eaten or drank anything. She had had water, at least.

"You should leave the sim," she said. "You've been in too long."

"I went back to the ship. It was dark, the lights were all out. I don't think we're going to make it if we don't wake the sleepers soon."

Why do I only ever have bad news? "The sleepers all left the Battery."

"I know." Taren kept his gaze trained on the other side of the bank. "There's only one way to wake them now. We need the tar you hid."

Lake stepped back from him. "No. We can't."

Taren turned to her, his gaze heavy with despair. "Tell me what you did with it. I know you brought it here the first time you left the Battery. I saw you."

"I don't have it. I tried to hide it but—"

"What's on your hand?"

Lake realized she was cradling her palm in her other hand.

The makeshift bandage had come off in the water, and now the mark on her palm showed plainly. Lake noticed with a deep, sinking feeling that it had spread past her wrist.

She expected Taren to back away, to protect himself. But he only gaped and said, "You have the box of tar?"

"No, they took it. I hid it but—"

"Show me where it is." Taren looked to the top of the waterfall as if he suspected that she'd left it behind when she'd jumped into the river. "Leave the sim, and I'll do it myself. You won't have to help."

Hadn't he heard her? Didn't he believe her? "They took it. Eden and her sleepers. They have it now. We have to find another way to wake them."

"Lake," Taren groaned. "There's no time. Please, just tell me where it is—"

"You don't understand." Lake's voice erupted from her throat. "It's *gone*. All of it. You think if you wake the sleepers you can go home, but that's gone too. I found the captain. He told me what happened: we left Earth. We can't go back." The words rushed out, a tidal force she could no longer contain. Home was gone. The yard Willow had hidden treasures in, the beach where they'd searched the tide pools. And more— things she could not think about now because they would drown her heart in regret.

Taren looked to Willow, as if for confirmation. She sat on the gravel bank, hunched in defeat, staring vacantly at the passing water. "You found the captain," Taren said to Lake, "in a simulated version of the ship."

Lake was too numb to respond.

"You went to the area of the sim where it's hardest to keep your grip on reality," Taren went on. "And now you think we left Earth? We headed into space, away from the only place we could be sure of for our survival?"

Lake studied the wet, shining gravel. The felted trees. "The captain said . . ." Had she found the captain? There had been a strange man, half-melded to the sim.

"You told me the captain died in stasis. You said you'd never seen the captain on the ship before."

Lake reeled. Taren held out a hand to steady her, careful to avoid her tar-stained arm. "Are you okay?" he asked.

Something moved in the gravel near Lake's feet: tar, oozing up from the rocks.

Lake looked up at Taren, pierced by his betrayal.

"Lake," he said, shaking his head, "I wasn't trying to—"

"Stay back!" She pulled out of his grip, still alarmed at the sight of the tar spreading over the gravel. Taren had done that—he'd confused her on purpose, to get more tar.

"Wait, listen," Taren pleaded.

Willow scrambled up from the ground. "What's going on?"

Lake moved to block her from Taren, and a new wave of dizziness overtook her. "Stay away from us." She held out her tarry palm in defense. She edged toward him, forcing him away from the tar bubbling over the gravel near their feet. *One push and he could send me into the tar.*

Would he do that?

She didn't know. She only knew that she felt sick and weak and confused.

"Lake," Taren said, and she looked up to see that he was

standing in the water, and she was too, and still she didn't feel safe from the tar on the bank.

"Keep going," she commanded.

Taren gave her a pleading look, but he backed away until the water came to his chest.

"Go to the other bank," Lake told him. "I'm going to find the sleepers. I don't want you to come with me."

Taren shivered in the water. "How will you wake them?"

He knew she didn't have an answer.

"Cross to the bank," Lake said. "Don't follow us."

She put her hand into the water. Tendrils of ink spread from her palm, and from the tar that now coated her arm like a gauntlet.

Taren jerked in alarm. He turned and swam to the opposite bank.

The ink spread. In a moment, the water looked as though it had fallen into shadow.

"Lake, what are you doing?" Taren called from the opposite bank. He looked over his shoulder, peering into the darkness. "I'm scared."

Lake stood in the late-afternoon light, looking into the darkness that gathered around Taren on the opposite bank. "I'm sorry," she said. "Don't follow us."

She beckoned to Willow and they turned and fled into the trees.

26

TAREN

Darkness at his back, Taren seethed. Cold through, shrouded in gloom. Betrayed.

Was it true what Lake had said—could they never return home? Or had the sim tricked her so it could keep her in its grasp forever?

Everything had its own will to survive. Lake did—a stronger will than Taren could ever have guessed. Taren did, a will so strong it frightened him. Maybe the sim did too.

But what if she's right? The thought clawed its way into Taren's fear-thickened brain. *What if we woke for nothing?*

What if he had come out of stasis just to witness the ship in its last throes? To face death fully awake, to watch the dark of deep space swallow him?

"She's wrong," he groaned. "She's wrong."

But he didn't know, and the confusion of it fogged his brain. He looked for the stars tattooed on his arm, trying to orient himself. They had been a constellation once: Taurus, the bull. The same constellation that marked his brother's arm.

"I didn't forget you." He said it to his brother, to his parents. To the house with the scuffed kitchen, and the stairway that overlooked the Pacific.

"I didn't forget you." He said it to himself, the only person he had left.

And even then, it sounded like a lie.

A figure appeared next to him, clutching its arm in the same way Taren clutched his own. Same hitched breathing, same dripping clothes.

"What should I do, Gray?" Taren asked. But the figment wasn't Gray.

It was a twin of Taren himself.

And the voice that answered from the darkness wasn't Gray's, either—it was the rumbling voice that had issued from the crater. *"You know what you need to do."*

Taren's breath shuddered in his lungs. Another twin appeared on his other side, bowed with the same misery he felt.

Fear and desperation bubbled in Taren, darker than tar. Another twin appeared on the bank, and another. Another.

Soon, a dozen figments stood clustered around Taren. Cold, determined. But hemmed by the poisoned river.

They watched the water flow past, tainted with tar. But already, the tar was diluting.

Soon, the water would run clear.

27

WILLOW

The trees with their shedding bark stood like robed figures, watching Willow and Lake stumble past.

"Lake, wait," Willow cried, and her sister reluctantly turned back.

The tar made a sickening glove over Lake's hand. It went halfway to her elbow. The sight of it washed Willow with terror. *She'll disappear.*

What will happen to me?

Lake waited for her to say something, to explain why she'd stopped. Willow thought her buckling knees must say it all.

"Will, we have to hurry."

She'll disappear, and I'll melt away into nothing.

Maybe Willow would turn to tar and seep through the system. Maybe that's what tar was, liquid code, ghost-matter. "I'm afraid," she said. "I—I need to hide."

Lake came close and put an arm around Willow's shoulders, though she kept her tar-covered hand angled away. "Hide?"

Ahead, the shelters loomed. Willow wished she could re-member the time she'd spent there with Lake. She tried to imagine sleeping under soft bark-hide. Eating sweet fruit. Not as good as root beer, but it must have been a nice life, even so.

And then—a creature had come. That's what the captain had told them. The gauzy-eyed captain, who made Willow lose all interest in air travel. Space travel was already ruined for her.

"You said to hide," Willow told Lake. She thought she could remember that, or at least that Lake had hidden some-thing. Willow knew more about hiding than most. She'd dug holes in her sim-yard, buried treasure inside. And she could hide herself, too, like she hid in the computer system when-ever Lake left the sim.

The important thing was to survive.

Lake leaned down to make herself level with Willow, in the way Willow hated. "What are you talking about, Will?"

But Lake wouldn't understand. Willow knew that she herself had hidden things, and buried things. Lake was still pretending she hadn't done the same.

She gave Willow a pained smile, and then picked up some-thing from the ground. "Look, it's the fruit we ate. Remember?" She brushed it off on her wet shirt and handed it to Willow, as if Willow were nothing but a child to be cheered up after a bad day.

Crackling footsteps sounded in the trees all around them.

Willow wasn't the only one good at hiding.

28

EDEN

Once, others had chosen who would survive. They chose who boarded ships, who sheltered in bunkers.

Once, others chose. Now, Eden did.

She chose who sheltered in the Battery, a safe place to hide. Everyone there had understood it wouldn't be their final home. They were all waiting—for what, they didn't always know. Eden knew. She'd had visions of a lost world, a place never tainted by ash and smoke.

Now, they claimed it.

They had found the shelters already waiting for them under the trees, as if reality had bent to Eden's will once again. While the others moved into the camp, Eden worked to dig a hole for the lead box now almost empty of tar. She had ordered her soldiers to destroy the slope that led down from the entrance to this world—so that her people would feel safe. But she'd heard rumors that the danger they thought they had escaped was already here waiting for them.

And now she knew the rumors were true: a girl emerged from the trees, surrounded by Eden's soldiers.

The Angel of Death.

She looked different from the last time Eden had seen her—but her sister looked the same.

Eden straightened as they approached. The lead box set into the hole at her feet felt to her like a yawning pit, a grave. She would be rid of the tar soon, and the past would be buried.

"Destroyer," Eden pronounced, and she saw the Angel flinch. "You brought death to the Battery. But *we* have the tar now."

She motioned to her soldiers, and they came one by one to scrape their weapons into the box of tar half-buried in the dirt at Eden's feet. When their sticks and metal struts rose from the box, tar clung to each like a spear-tip.

"This is the last of the tar," Eden told the Angel. "With it, I destroy death."

The Angel moved in front of her sister, shielding her. "I came to tell you—please just let me tell you first. Or do you already know? You've been to this place before."

The shelters had been waiting for them when they arrived. But then, Eden had found the Battery to be much the same way. It had unfolded itself to her as she entered. She had dreamed of it as a shelter-city, full of food and blankets and clothes, and it had become one.

And yet, she had seen *this* place long before she'd come to it. She knew the sounds these trees made in the wind, she knew the cinnamon smell of unfurling bark.

"Do you remember?" the Angel asked, and she lifted her hand.

Eden's soldiers surged toward her, but Eden called, "Wait."

In the Angel's outstretched hand sat a small globe of fruit.

Eden touched the locket around her neck, a tiny gold globe.

The sweet tang of fruit came back to her—not just the smell, but the taste. She had tasted this fruit. She had eaten it in a snug shelter that glowed with afternoon light. She had shared it at a makeshift table laid out in the middle of camp. Its juice had stained her clothes, had watered the dirt, had brought the birds down from the trees.

How could it be? She had lived here before.

Her soldiers knew it too. They stared at the fruit in the Angel's hand and lifted their gazes to the trees and looked to Eden like newborn creatures blinking against the light.

Yes, we lived here. We were happy here. And then . . .

"We all lived here together," Lake said, echoing Eden's thoughts. "These shelters were ours. But a creature attacked and chased us out." She tensed suddenly, her gaze locked on something behind Eden.

Eden turned. The shelter behind her glowed softly in the light filtering through the canopy. Except for one dark spot along its side.

A vision came to Eden, an image of the future: her soldiers clashing with a shadowy enemy, slashing with their tar-tipped weapons, destroying the shelters. Issuing death into an unspoiled world.

Only it wasn't a vision of the future.

It was a memory of the past.

Eden stepped toward the shelter and pulled back the ruined

bark covering. It was as if she were splitting open a piece of rotten fruit: inside, a great mass of tar roiled.

They had lived here once. Not soldiers, or queens. Ordinary people. Destroyed by conflict.

"Drop your weapons," she said, not a command but a quiet plea. The sticks and struts fell to the dirt.

Eden backed from the shelter as the images played again through her head. She pressed her hands to her mouth, stifling a cry that was building in her throat.

Behind her, the Angel said, "A terrible creature . . ."

But they both knew: it had not been a creature that had ruined this place.

Her soldiers gathered close around her to see the roiling tar. Now came noises from the trees that made Eden turn in confusion. *Who's out there?*

A dozen figures crept out from behind the trunks. Somehow, they all had the same face.

They picked up the weapons Eden's soldiers had dropped.

The same face, and each one angry.

29

TAREN

The sleepers scattered. Taren moved forward, and the figments of himself moved with him. Misery was a cold cloak weighting his river-wet shoulders.

"Tell yourself they're figments if it helps," he said to his figments as he watched the sleepers stream from the shelters and flee into the woods. "Tell yourself they won't survive if we don't wake them."

He knew he was really telling himself.

"Do you want to survive?" he asked.

The figments were restless, eager to attack.

The question was only for himself.

They surged forward, and Taren couldn't tell if he was surging with them or watching them attack. He felt he'd been split into pieces, and none of the pieces were his any longer.

Shouts of frightened sleepers rang through the air, but Taren heard them as if through a tunnel. At the corners of his vision, he saw figments swinging their weapons, saw sleepers fall to the dirt. A sleeper darted out from a shelter, and Taren followed on instinct.

The sleeper saw him, stumbled, fell. Taren lurched toward him.

The boy turned, still on the ground, and gaped up at the tar clinging to the stick Taren held over him. He was skinny, small, Willow's age. Just a kid. Taren's arm locked in place. It refused to lower the weapon he held.

Do you want to survive? The rock-and-dirt voice of the crater.

Do you want to survive? Taren's own voice, echoing in his head.

Taren searched himself for an answer. *I did survive. I got on the ship.*

He didn't know if he could do more.

A blur of movement caught his attention, made him turn. A figment stalked toward him, eyeing the boy on the ground. It so unsettled Taren to see his face on the figment that for a moment he could only stare.

The figment pointed his weapon toward the boy on the ground, ready to paint him with tar.

The movement jolted Taren out of his stupor. Where he had been unsure, he was now certain. He couldn't let this boy die suffocated by confusion and fear. "No," he said to the figment, "wait."

The figment ignored him. It lunged.

Taren lunged too. He jammed his stick into the figment's gut, and then watched the twin of himself stumble back and collapse into the dirt.

The tar began to spread, seeping into the figment's shirt, crawling over the arms clutched over the figment's stomach, moving up its chest, its neck. Taren gaped in horror. He felt as if he were looking in a mirror, watching himself die. He dropped his weapon.

Two other figments stopped what they were doing, sensing a threat. They came to watch their fallen twin writhe in the dirt while the tar swallowed it. Then they looked up at Taren, the offender. Threat to their survival.

They stalked toward him.

"Wait," he said. "Stop."

He backed away from them. But a third figment closed in, a fourth.

They pointed their weapons toward him.

One of them spoke: "Tell yourself they're figments." Repeating what Taren had said earlier.

Fear knifed through Taren. He held out his hands, but he knew they were no shield against tar.

"Tell yourself they won't survive," another figment said.

"Unless we wake them," Taren finished.

They closed in, and Taren could only hope that after, he would wake.

30

LAKE

The cries and shouts of sleepers followed Lake through the trees, and the crash of the figments slashing through shelters. "Where are we going?" Willow gasped as she ran.

Away.

Fast.

But the sleepers . . .

Lake stopped and pulled Willow behind a tree. They looked back to see the army of figments chasing sleepers from the shelters, and slashing sleepers with their tar-tipped spears.

Lake couldn't stop staring at the figments, each with Taren's face. She didn't know if one of them had been Taren himself. Was he hunting sleepers with the rest of them?

He'd lost himself to the sim. She should have never brought him back with her.

He'd been alone too long in that tiger yard. If she had rescued him sooner, would everything have been different? Or if she had gotten the sleepers off the ship long ago? She'd chosen to work slowly, to wake the sleepers one by one where she had to. Even when she felt time running short.

I made my choices.

Taren made his.

"We have to get the sleepers to follow us," Lake told Willow. "We have to get them out of here."

She couldn't tear her gaze from the camp, where the figments painted sleepers with tar.

I've seen this before.

Long ago, when she'd lived in this pocket of the sim—chaos and fear had erupted then, too. It had started when people kept vanishing from camp. Awakening from the sim, Lake realized now. Fear had spread like a shadow, confusion like a cloud. And then—

Tar bubbling through the bark of the trees, shouts piercing the air.

Lake and Willow had escaped through the forest. They'd looked back at camp like they were doing now, taking in a last glimpse of the fray. Lake had been close enough to see their faces.

And one of those faces—

She could see it now, so clear in her memory. The face of a boy holding a spear tipped in tar.

No. It's not true—

"Lake?" Willow said, breaking through her thoughts. "Lake, we have to go," Willow pleaded.

Lake nodded, fought back the nausea that threatened to overtake her. Her gaze roved the trees, searching for sleepers who'd managed to escape. She had to find a way to lead them out of here, out of the sim.

She spotted Eden, flanked by two of her soldiers. "Hey!" Lake called.

Eden spotted her, motioned to her soldiers.

"We'll take them toward the waterfall," Lake told Willow. "We'll cut a door in the rock."

Eden's soldiers scrambled to gather the sleepers running from camp. But now the figments were following, chasing them through the trees. Lake pushed away all thoughts of anything but escape, and pulled Willow into a run.

They came to the waterfall now, but the figments were so close behind that Lake could see their flashing eyes when she looked back. There was no time to cut a doorway. They had to hide.

"Cross the river," she called. "Into the darkness. It's our only chance to evade them."

One of Eden's guards pulled off the goggles slung around his neck and handed them to her. "Infrared. They'll help you see in the dark."

"What will you use?" Lake asked him.

"I'll follow you," he said. "We all will. We'll form a chain once we get across the river."

Lake nodded. She turned and dove into the water and came out on the opposite bank, into deep gloom.

"Willow?"

"Here."

Lake put on the goggles, and Willow became an orange flame in her infrared vision.

And something else caught Lake's attention, a fainter glow from up on the rocky slope. The outline of a doorway in the darkness.

How?

Someone had carved a door there. Taren? Was that how he'd gotten here to the lost world?

It didn't matter—it was a way out.

More flaming silhouettes were emerging from the river, sleepers desperate to hide. "Follow my voice," Lake called. "Take each other's hands."

They found her in the darkness and she helped them up the rocky slope, nudging them in the right direction as they passed her. She saw the figments emerge from the river too, the tar on their spears glowing in the infrared vision her goggles lent her. They paced at the edge of the darkness, but they had lost sight of their prey.

Some of the other sleepers wore goggles like Lake's and they helped her lead the way to the door. But when Lake finally stepped close to it, she saw that it *wasn't* a doorway—at least, not any longer. The pocket on the other side must have closed, because the doorway had filled in. Tar still showed along the arc that had once formed the top of the doorway, but below was only a dark, solid wall.

I can make another doorway. Lake lifted her tar-covered hand. It ached, constricted by the tightening grip of the tar. She ignored the pain. Envisioned the ship.

She traced the arc of a doorway. Traced an X through the wall.

The darkness crumbled.

"It's time to leave," Lake said to the sleepers who blinked in the light shining through the opening cracks.

"Back to the Battery?" Eden asked.

"No." *To the ship. And then—*"Someplace new."

Eden shuffled closer to the doorway. She reached hesitantly to touch the widening cracks in the disintegrating wall. Darkness seemed to fall away under her touch as pieces of the wall dropped. The other sleepers pushed forward, as if sensing escape at last. The air went electric with anticipation.

Lake quailed. She backed from the doorway. Because even though escape would halt the spread of poison now spreading down her entire left side, and even though it would allow her to finally leave a broken ship and find a home—

It also meant leaving Willow.

"You can't go," Willow said, clutching for her in the dark. "You're leaving me."

Lake smelled smoke, felt fire in her veins. A great weight seemed to be hurtling down from above and threatening to press her deep underground. "I never wanted to leave," she said. "I never wanted to leave you behind."

Willow pawed at her arm. "I'm here, and you're leaving me."

"But you're not here." Lake choked back her despair. "Willow's not really here. I left her back on Earth."

"But you didn't."

Lake pulled out of Willow's grip. She knew what was happening. She was falling deep into the sim's delusion, following Willow past the point of escape.

"I'm inside the sim," Willow said. "I got on the ship. Don't you remember? You didn't leave me behind."

Lake bit her lip. *If only, if only.* "That's not true. You're a figment. You appear, you disappear."

"I'm a figment. But the real Willow is here. She's here in the sim."

In the distance, an eerie cry rose. The call of the creature hiding in the darkness.

But there is no creature. The captain was wrong—it wasn't a creature who drove us from this place. We did that ourselves. The ruined shelter had been proof of that.

The cry rose again. But this time, Lake realized it wasn't a creature calling to her. It was a voice.

And it sounded like Willow's.

31

LAKE

The voice called again, a cry carried by the wind. Willow's voice.

And yet Willow stood here before her, silent in the darkness.

Lake knew what was happening: the sim didn't want to let her go. It had her in its claws, and it was digging in.

But she had to follow the voice. Because what if it was true—what if Willow really had gotten onto the ship? What if Willow's figment was standing here in front of Lake, and the real Willow was calling to her from somewhere in the distance?

You know Willow didn't get on the ship. The sim is tricking you.

Lake had been in the sim too long. Or returned too many times. The sim knew and it was playing with her mind.

But she still had to go.

"Wait here, Will," Lake said.

The figment of Willow turned to watch as Lake passed, even in the pitch darkness.

Lake stumbled over rocks, made her way to a pebbled shore where the crash of waves all but drowned out the voice still calling from the distance: *Laaaaake.* A long, eerie cry, pulling at the very core of her heart.

Willow. The real Willow. She's calling for help.

"Willow!" Lake called into the wind.

The voice rose again, carried on an icy blast of ocean air. Through her goggles, Lake could see a fiery silhouette far in the distance.

Willow, trapped on the ice cap at the far edge of the ocean.

Could it be?

Lake stumbled forward, gasping in shock when her boots plunged into freezing water.

How do I get to her?

Before her, the dark ocean was full of life. Small flecks of yellow flitted at the surface of the dark water. Strange webs of red veins winked in and out of existence, rising in the water and sinking again. Lake trudged through the freezing water, drawing in great shuddering breaths while her muscles threatened to lock. A red web flexed before her, and now she could make out the dim outline of a massive shell.

She didn't think, just clambered onto the shell, out of the terrible water. Her fingers found the horned edge at the front of the sea creature's shell, and she willed her numb hands to hold on.

In the water before her, more spots of yellow flicked this way and that. The shelled creature surged after them, chasing its prey.

"No," Lake said, "go to the ice."

She'd kept her tar-covered arm held out, away from the sea creature, but now she saw how it glowed in the same way that the tiny fish in the water did. She held her hand out before the sea creature like a lure. Its head rose in the water, a yellowish shape through Lake's goggles. She held her hand out before it, steering it toward where the figure still called from the ice.

The yellow silhouette in the distance grew larger as Lake drew closer to the shelf of ice. Lake shivered and groaned in the cold. She tried to make herself warmer just by willing it. She kept her eyes glued to Willow's form as the sea creature ferried her closer. Strange, though, how different Willow looked through the goggles. Not so wiry.

In fact, not very small at all.

And if Lake gave in to the uneasy feeling that had been growing inside her, she would have to turn the creature, to stop it from taking her ever closer to the shelf of ice.

Because the person in the distance was not Willow.

It was a boy, or a man—tall, with broad shoulders.

Lake felt as though she had slid into the black sea and frozen in its depths. Willow was not out on that ice. The man was alone.

Lake hesitated, her arm held high above the water. Out on the ice shelf, the figure stood just as still.

Ice formed at the back of her throat, at the edges of her heart.

What do I do?

The figure called to her. But the wind pulled at the sound

so that Lake couldn't make it out. Was he calling her name? Calling for help?

Or was his call a warning?

She started to shake so hard she had to crouch lower on the sea creature's shell to keep from falling into the water.

Why would someone be out here on the ice, all alone?

The only person who had been to the dark half of the lost world was Taren.

Taren—and his figments.

The sea creature bumped against something in the dark: the shelf of ice. Lake watched the figure in the distance. It could be a figment. But what if it was a sleeper, trapped with no way out?

Lake climbed off the sea creature and onto the ice. She opened her mouth to call to the person not twenty feet away, but she couldn't bring herself to do it. She was trembling all over, cold and afraid. The tar that coated her arm and her side had traveled down her back now, and she felt it drawing tight like a second skin. The sim had lured her out here, into darkness, and now she was trapped. She should have walked through that door with the others, to the ship and safety.

Why couldn't it have been Willow out here on the ice?

She had left Willow behind. Now it was only her and a stranger.

A sleeper or a figment. Wanting rescue—or violence.

She crept toward the figure, her steps heavy with dread. "Hello?" she said, but her voice died on the wind.

It's a figment, a trap.

She'd left Taren in the dark once, trapped and alone. She'd

had to—to keep herself safe. Was this person like him, seething and dangerous?

Or was he like the boy she'd found alone in a tiger yard, waiting for rescue?

The figure was hunched, shivering, its arms wrapped around itself. A sleeper, cold and miserable. Lake was close enough now that she could almost reach out and touch it. "Hello?" she said again, and this time the figure heard her. It lurched back, afraid. The movement sent lightning through Lake. She held out her arm, the tar like a glove of fire in her vision.

The figure was breathing as hard as she was, its chest heaving. It inched toward her, blinded by darkness. Lake kept her arm out like a shield. Cold and fear were jaws locking around her heart. She was afraid to speak again, afraid the figure would know where she was. Any moment it would pounce, but she was too frightened to move.

The tar tightened around her arm, moved along her shoulders, sizzled on her back.

How can it hurt me? I'm nearly dead.

She lowered her arm as the figure moved closer. "Don't be afraid," she said, and didn't know if she said it to the figure or to herself.

"Lake." The figure lurched forward, but this time, Lake wasn't afraid—she knew that voice.

"Ransom."

He fell toward her, and she had to brace him with her unmarked arm. His skin was ice. "I made a door. It took me here." His teeth chattered so that he could hardly speak. "I couldn't get back. I don't know how long I've been out here—a long time, I think."

She looked over his shoulder and saw it in the distance: the faint outline of a doorway carved with tar. Through her goggles, the tar showed red. But to Ransom, it would be invisible in the dark.

"Come on," she said, gripping his arm with her good hand. "Let's get you out of here."

They struggled over the ice, Ransom stumbling and silent, Lake doing her best to move even as the tar gripped tighter over her skin, numbed her muscles. They somehow made it to the door, and then could only collapse together onto a bench-seat, weak from cold.

"I was calling so long," Ransom said. "I didn't think any-one would come for me."

"I didn't know it was you calling out," Lake said. "I thought it was . . ." Lake closed her eyes. Her relief at bringing Ransom to safety was quickly fading, giving way to something heavier. "I left Willow. I didn't say goodbye."

Why did I think it was her on the ice?

I was so desperate to save her.

"I'm sorry," Ransom said.

She could go and find Willow now and say goodbye—Willow's figment, all Lake had of her sister. But was there time? The tar was seeping through her shirt. She could hear it eating the wall behind her. If she didn't leave the sim, it would soon swallow her.

The only thing that kept her here was her fear that the tar

wouldn't leave her when she went back to the ship. She'd seen the mark it had left last time. Would she recover from that?

She turned to look at Ransom and was relieved to find he was already warming, like she was. Coming back to life now that he was back in his pub. She traced her thumb over his jaw, trying to memorize the lines of his face. And asking herself a question at the same time . . .

"Did you know about the planet?"

The pained look in his eye sent a dagger through her heart. "Every time I tried to tell you, you'd bury yourself deeper in the sim. I was afraid you'd never come out."

She moved her hand down to grip his. "Maybe it would have been too much for me, to find out we'd left Earth."

"The sim was supposed to help all the sleepers get ready to go to the planet. But something happened . . ." He dropped his head. "With the tar."

"I know."

He shook his head, as if he thought she didn't understand.

"Everyone left, ran away," Lake said. "They pushed themselves into their own pockets of the sim. They forgot about everything except their nightmares of what we left behind on Earth."

"What we left behind," Ransom echoed dully. "*Did* we leave it behind? Terrible things happened in the lost world."

She let go of his hand. "I remember."

He looked up, alarm in his eyes.

"I know what you did," Lake told him. "A long time ago. When we all lived together in the lost world."

He dropped his head again. His arm trembled against hers.

"You aren't a figment, are you?" Lake said. She was shaking now too, overwhelmed by the pain showing on his downturned face, at the grief bruising her heart. "I thought that was why you would never tell me anything about yourself. I thought that was why you never left the sim. But I was wrong."

His shadowed gaze, in his dark moods—they weren't evidence of frustration.

They were proof of his shame.

"You're just another sleeper," Lake said. "You lived in the lost world with us. Until . . ."

"The tar." He leaned away from her. "I was trying to defend myself. But it doesn't matter—I'll never get free of what I did."

Lake's arm throbbed under the thin layer of tar. Her heart felt just as sore.

She'd never used tar on anyone—but she'd used it to defend herself. She'd used it to taint the river and keep Taren trapped for a while. So she could understand, at least a little, why Ransom had used it.

And she could see his regret mapped on his face.

She touched his bowed back. "I have to go. Come with me?"

He turned at her touch, but his gaze was still heavy. "I don't deserve to go."

An old longing surprised Lake: she wished for the sight she'd seen through the view-screen windows of the eatery, the blue curve of Earth. She wished she could give Ransom that sight, to remind him of what they'd once had, a home they hadn't earned and could never reclaim.

"None of us does," she said.

Who could deserve something as vast and beautiful as a planet, or even a tree, or a single blade of grass?

"Give me one last chance at giving you a gift?" she asked.

Ransom looked around the empty pub at the scarred wood of the bar, the carpet of broken glass. Lake turned his face with her good hand, leaned in carefully, conscious of the pain crackling over her poisoned skin. Kissed him like she had the first time, like she was sure she'd know him forever, and he still tasted like salt water.

She pressed into Ransom's hand the coin she had taken from his pocket, the one with the tree from the lost world.

"This was already mine," he told her with a weak smile.

"You lost it," she reminded him. "Now I'm giving it back to you."

The hardness in his eyes melted. He closed his fingers around the coin. "Is it as simple as that?"

Lake swallowed against the pain in her arm and all down her back. "I'm afraid," she admitted. "We left one war behind, and we started another in the sim. I wish I had one reason to believe we won't do the same thing on the planet."

Ransom squeezed the coin in his fist. "What about this: I was trapped on the ice, and you were scared. But you saved me anyway."

Lake's heart flooded with warmth. She pressed her hand against Ransom's cheek.

"You've been so afraid," Ransom went on. "That's what's been keeping you trapped here."

Lake shook her head. "Trapped?"

"In the sim."

He was confused. He was losing his sense of reality. "I'm not the one who's been trapped in the sim, Ransom. *You* are."

"Only because I don't want to leave you," he said.

She studied his earnest expression and could find no trace of confusion there. And yet, what he was saying made no sense.

"You told me once that Willow likes to bury things," he went on. "I don't think she's the only one."

"What are you talking about?" *He means me. He thinks I buried something.* "What is it you think I buried?"

A voice called from the distance, muffled by the pub's door. Lake's head snapped up. "Willow?"

Ransom looked between Lake and the door.

"Did you hear that?" Lake asked him. *Or am I imagining it?*

Ransom's gaze turned hopeful. "You're starting to remember, aren't you?"

Again, the voice came from behind the door. Calling to her as it had on the ice. *Laaaake.*

This isn't real. It's the sim.

But the echo of that voice pulled her up from the bench, away from Ransom, toward the door.

Someone had already marked it with an X. Had it been her? She couldn't remember. If she opened the door, would she find Willow on the other side, or only the ship?

Laaaaaake, came the voice.

Lake opened the door and hurtled through.

32

LAKE

Hum of machines. Roar of her own breath. And the ritual she knew well: confusion, dread, the sinking realization that she was alone.

She pushed herself out of the stasis bed. Stumbled out of the chamber.

Why is it so dark?

Voices in the dark warehouse, the whispers and groans of sleepers newly awakened. Shouldn't some strain have been lifted from the ship's systems? But the lights were still off, the air still thin.

She found her way out of the warehouse, fumbling along with hands outstretched. A single electric flare lit the hallway.

A voice called to her. *Lake.*

Lake lurched toward the door the voice had come through, a door she must have tried a hundred times before. Locked. Always locked. Like so many other doors on this ship.

But Willow was in there. She was calling . . .

Lake.

This couldn't be happening. She had left the sim. Her mind was cracking under the strain of being under so long.

In the light from the flare, the skin along her arm showed ashy gray. Lake lost her breath. She could feel the same deadened skin all down her side, over her back, across her shoulders. The tar hadn't left her.

"Lake." The voice was close now, just on the other side of the door she had her back pressed against.

Stop, don't listen.

It's not Willow. She can't be here.

She looked down at the thread on her wrist, the one that never changed, inside the sim or out. The sight of it made her shake all over, and she tried to understand why.

"Willow likes to bury things. I don't think she's the only one."

Lake pictured Willow kneeling in the grass of their yard at home, spreading dirt over buried treasure. The same thing she did every time Lake found her in that corner of the sim. What had she buried?

She tried to remember that day—the real day on Earth. A long time ago. Willow had showed her the treasure, hadn't she?

She'd held out her palm to Lake, and there lay two bracelets of knotted blue thread. *"They're for us,"* she told Lake. But when Lake had reached to take one, Willow pulled her hand away. She wanted to bury them, like she did with all her special treasures. *"I like knowing there's a secret under the dirt,"* she'd said. *"I like that there's something in the world that only I know about."*

Lake had smiled as Willow had dropped them into a tin. And then she'd watched Willow kneel in the grass and bury the tin.

She buried them. So how am I wearing one on my wrist?

Lake turned to the door. She touched the handle. Pushed. The door opened.

All this time . . .

She trembled. *All this time, I've been in the sim. Even here on the ship.*

Only ever in the sim.

And is it possible . . .

Has Willow been here in the sim-ship, waiting for me?

She stepped through the door.

Beyond lay a room like so many on the ship: metal walls gleaming dully in the low light, cool metal floor. But here was a bed with a green bedspread, and grass-green rug to match. A small table, a single chair.

And sitting in the chair—

Willow.

For a moment, Lake could only stare, stunned. Could it really be her? Was it Willow, or only a figment?

Willow's face was lined with uncertainty. "You said to hide. You said it wasn't safe, and I should hide here until you came for me."

Lake stepped closer, peered down into Willow's upturned face. "I said that?"

Willow nodded.

"But how can you be here?" Lake asked. "You never even got on the ship."

"I did. They let younger siblings come along."

"They said they would but—"

Lake touched Willow's cheek, her pointed chin. She smoothed her messy hair back from her face. *Is she real?*

She remembered the shelter under the trees where Willow had slept in the bed beside hers. Where they'd eaten fruit at a little table, and Willow had made a game with the pits. She remembered hiding with Willow under soft bark blankets when the sharp sounds of arguments came from outside. And running with her, when the shouting turned to violence.

She remembered bringing Willow here, to their pocket in the sim. A pocket that looked just like the ship, but never came any closer to bringing them home.

"You left me here," Willow said. "I've been waiting for you."

Lake dropped to her knees. "I was afraid. I didn't want you to get hurt."

"Then why didn't we ever leave the sim? Why didn't we go back to the real ship?"

Because I'm still afraid.

I'm afraid because if we leave the ship, there will be no going back.

I'm afraid that what happened in the sim will happen on the planet.

She must not have known, when she'd first come to this corner of the sim, that it wasn't really the ship. She must have thought she had escaped the sim, when in fact, she'd only made it larger.

All those sleepers I thought I'd wakened—I only brought them here, to another pocket in the sim.

And if I wake now?

They would wake too. Every last one.

Even Willow would wake.

If Willow is real.

Lake wanted to throw her arms around Willow, carry her through the door, take her back to the real ship that had been waiting for them so long. She wanted so much for Willow to be real.

"I want to go," Willow said.

Lake pulled Willow's jacket onto her shoulder. "I know, Will."

Willow slipped it right back off.

Lake let out a sound halfway between a laugh and cry. She was more afraid now than ever. Afraid that if she left the sim, Willow wouldn't follow. Afraid that if Willow did, it would only be to the same conflict and chaos they'd found in the sim.

We can't escape ourselves.

She looked down at the gray skin covering her arm. *Angel of Death.*

"I'm hungry," Willow said.

"There isn't any . . ." Lake's voice trailed off. The ship was only a simulation, and she could make it what she wanted. Couldn't she?

She closed her hand into a tight fist. Then she opened her fingers.

A bright globe of fruit sat on her palm.

Willow marveled at it. "Where did you get that?"

Lake couldn't take her eyes from it, even as she gave it to Willow. "There'll be more, in the place we're going."

Willow bit into the fruit, and the sweet smell filled the

air. Lake almost couldn't enjoy it for the anxiety twisting her stomach. *Angel of Death.*

But I'm not an angel.

"Are we finally going?" Willow asked.

Lake studied her, uncertain. She didn't know if this was goodbye.

She stood and pulled Willow up from the chair. "Yes. We're going."

Lake traced an X on the door with her finger, turned the handle, and ushered Willow through while her heart nearly burst with hoping.

33

LAKE

Lake woke. Alone as always.

She lifted the lid over her bed and then froze, startled by the sight of her unmarked skin. The stain of the tar had vanished. No gray skin. She went dizzy with relief, and then confusion. She was still struggling to wake from the deepest dream she'd ever had.

She struggled out of the bed, weak and unsteady. Her stomach empty and cramping, her mouth dry. She leaned against the wall, gathering her strength. Too many thoughts were crashing through her head, but one escaped through her lips. "Please don't let me be alone here."

She finally managed to slide the door of the chamber aside.

There was Ransom, leaning against the wall, blinking at her with the startled gaze of a newborn creature.

"Ransom? I thought..." Lake pulled him into her, wrapped her arms around his waist. Pressed her head into the hollow of his shoulder. He seemed no different from before.

She watched his pulse beat in his neck, listened to the hum of his breathing. Same boy who brought her shells on the beach, who built bridges out of toothpicks, who played imaginary pianos.

"I told you," he said, "I wasn't stuck in the sim. You were."

"But you were always there." *To be with* me, she realized. *And to hide from his guilt at whatever had happened in the lost world.* "And you always had such a hard time moving through the sim."

"Going back into the sim is harder than you think." He cracked a smile. "Everyone's heading to the shuttles. I already sent out a beacon to the government ships. They should be able to follow us here. The shuttles are stocked with supplies to hold us over on the surface of the planet until then."

"You've been busy."

"When I wasn't sleeping." His smile was easy for once.

Lake let go of him. "Is she here?"

But she could tell from his hesitation that he didn't know.

And then, from down the row of stasis chambers, a voice called, "Lake?"

Lake turned. A million suns rose inside her. "Willow."

In the shuttle, Lake clasped her hand around Willow's. The planet filled their view-screen: A swath of purple-blue, marbled by white clouds.

A new world.

Bright in the light of its star. Bright as a gem, a treasure that pressed them into silence. *A gift,* Lake thought, coming fully awake for the first time since her long sleep in the sim.

A gift more weighty than any she'd ever received.

She squeezed Willow's hand. *We're so lucky, Will.*

So lucky, and so very, very rich.

ACKNOWLEDGMENTS

Thank you to . . .

My editor, Ali Fisher, whose guidance and insight helped me find the most interesting territory this story had to offer.

My agent, Ammi-Joan Paquette, who helps me navigate the maze of publishing and believes in my most labyrinthine ideas.

My tireless team at Tor, in particular Devi Pillai, Saraciea Fennell, Becky Yeager, Liana Krissoff, Rafal Gibek, Steven Bucsok, Lesley Worrell for the jacket design, and everyone else who worked to make this story into a book.

Launch Pad Astronomy Workshop, where I learned so much more than I was able to fit into this story, and SFWA for funding my participation in the workshop. Also to Charles Hotchkiss for consulting on some of the scientific aspects of this story. (Any mistakes are my own.)

All those who offered story critiques and helped me find my way out of tricky plot corners, including Emily Henry, Traci Chee, Danielle Behr, and Gwynne Breidenstein.

My local writing friends, whose support keeps me going, particularly Stacey Lee, Kelly Loy Gilbert, and Randy Ribay, along with the rest of my local writing community, whose friendship means so much to me.

My local Bay Area bookstores, especially Hicklebee's, for promoting my books and also for being great places to hang out in.

My family, especially Jason and Toby Peevyhouse, for being awesome.